C. Osborne Ward

The Great Rebellion

Reminiscences of the Struggle that cost a million Lives

C. Osborne Ward

The Great Rebellion
Reminiscences of the Struggle that cost a million Lives

ISBN/EAN: 9783337210472

Printed in Europe, USA, Canada, Australia, Japan

Cover: Foto ©Andreas Hilbeck / pixelio.de

More available books at **www.hansebooks.com**

THE GREAT

REBELLION,

REMINISCENCES

OF THE

STRUGGLE THAT COST

A MILLION LIVES.

A DRAMA.

IN FIVE ACTS.

By C. Osborne Ward.

NEW YORK,

1881.

PLAY

of the

GREAT REBELLION.

INTRODUCTION.

SCENE *in a Sangamon forest.* LINCOLN *with axe, maul and wedge, splitting rails.*

LIN. ONE of the sweetest fruits of labor is
An honest living. I'd rather have
A homely crust, well earned, to nibble, washed
With a beverage of pure conscience down;
It's more refreshing, in my simple judgment,
Than the fruits of golden India, to the palate
Of the gouty millionaire who financiers regardless
Of ways and means of getting, save t'insure
The gotten. He's not a pauper who eats
This crust with relish; paupers are not the workers.
But he's the bone and sinew of the land;
He, on whom depends our boasted Yankee
Nation, for all her great developments. [*Works.*

Enter JOE, THE HUNTER, *at a distance.*

JOE. [*Scanning.*] Wal, I'd jest like ter know what on airth that mought be! My own mother allus teached me as how I was the ogliest creetur livin'; an' somehow I've got ter hatin' beauty, ogliness too; besides, my father has often 'jined it on me to shoot the fust man I ever see humlier'n me; and I tuk a vow one day when Sal Simmins gin me a ticket of everlastin' leave jest kase I war'nt good lookin' I tuk a vow I'd do it; an' I would long ago but I'd made up my mind the human race was putty safe for all my bullets; [*laughing*] for. hunt the wide world over, I haint got no comparison. I've kep' this ere old glass these ten year, 'an never looked in it on'y when I thought I seed critturs that 'ud stan' some fag along side uv my reflexion; but gosh! I've got an equal here. T'aint human tho'. Whew! My word's good. Yen thing's humblier'n me; I bleve I'll shoot. Hit's suthin' whether base, divine or middlin'. Base things is evil sperits, or devils; an' ef that ar' proves one on 'em, I sartain shant do any harm to rid the world on 'im; at least I'll make the ventur. Divine things is heavenly! That is, I spose they allus behave tharselves. They never drink whiskey, never swar, nor steal rats, nor minks, nor any other varmints out uv each other's traps. They live in a place they call Paradise, 'an its mighty oncommon thar visits on the airth, for they cant take no plunder back. an' mere visitin'! T'aint very likely they'r a goin' to the trouble ter visit us mortals. At least, I never had any on 'em come ter see me. They aint made uv blood and bones like us. They're sperits; that is, they're bladders like, stuffed with this yer hygroggin gas, and painted up to look like somebody. But I'm an idee ef that ar's one on 'em. the artix what painted 'im must uv had a right smart uv a rangertang fur a model ter daub arter. If its one uv that kind uv on-created varmints, an' I should slide a decider in 'im from my old wolf slayer here an' it should plunk a hole through his hide, the gas 'ud 'scape, he'd wilt or vanish in a twinklin' uv a cat's eye at a bull dog. Then thar's the middlin' kind uv thing that's human, an' I'll confess I'd rather blow a ball at any one uv the other above mentioned critters. I say, I feel a leetle squeamish about this thing; howsomever Huntin' Joe's not the man to break his promise. I'll shoot, hit or miss. [*Aims and snaps.*]

Lin. [*Startled, approaches* Joe.] Hello, old fellow. Hello you! What game is that you're sighting? It seems to me your piece is pointing too Directly on a line with me for safety.

Hun. [*Aside.*] Wal thar! I'm a little 'shamed uv this, a'ready. Hello, Longsplice, another jiffy an' y'd a been a dish for worms!

Lin. How's that?

Hun. How's that!

Lin. Do you take me for game?

Hun. Yes, *my* game I've been this ten year hunt-in' fur the like uv ye. My ole dad long sence made me swar I'd shoot the fust man I found oglier lookin' than me; an' at last I bleve I've found 'im. [*Scanning his glass.*]

Lin. Well, if I'm any uglier than you are blaze away.

Hun. Would yer be willin' to call it a tie?

Lin. I'm willing to call it a tie if it will turn your notion, or stay bloodshed; not that I feel my-self particularly worthy of a longer lease of life, but really, I do not think my offense merits capital punishment. My dear Sir, you have allowed an idea to deprave you; and the sentiment taught you by your father had well nigh worked your ruin.

We have other things to live for.   Give me
Your hand my friend, and vow a contra-vow :
That you will never let this whim of beauty
And its counterpart control your passions.
Let me convince you.   What is beauty ?
I own my gaunt, long legs and bony frame
And fingers, do not suit the silly whims
Of those Heaven graceful finishes in contour,
With form and feature faultless, with symmetry
In buoyant youth as perfect as the fawn.
A little time, a bruise, cut, cancer, or
A stroke of small pox, scar, or anything
May ruin all this beauty.   The great
Creator who in wisdom made us all,
Has doubtless made all perfect.   'Tis not for
Outward loveliness that we are valued.
A deed of kindness of the tongue, or hand,
May change the ugliest shape and features too,
Such as before were seen but to repel;
And cause a shrug of withering disgust
To startle spleeny natures, to forms superb.
'Tis by acts we're valued, by those possessed
Of sense sufficient to be worth a notice.
Who can esteem the judgment of a man
Who sets dumb visions and blind imagery
Against the sober, though battered and time
Worn walls of solid worth ?

HUN.   Wal, now, who'd a thought I was shootin' a man what could convince me out uv an idee I
was well nigh born with?   I say feller woodsman,
sence I've got older, I've often cogertated on the
same sort uv theery you're a preachin'; an' ef yer
call little childers folks, an' I've got ter thinkin' ole
folks is more onsensible'n they; ef yer call 'em folks
I say, I'll go halves with yer an' indorse yer idees;
fur I've lived long enough to know that this here

kentry's full uv wild cats an' more on em's got two legs than four; but I've tuk a right smart uv a liken' to you, 'cause yer seem to have the sensible simplicity uv a baby.

LIN. Why what do you mean by that?

HUN. What do I mean? I mean they're more good natered, like, eh! Hit's mighty few uv these 'ere growdupers as know thar's sich a critter livin' as huntin' Joe, 'cept to make mouths at. But y'd ori ter see the difference when I happen by Jack Farlan's clearin'. Hit sometimes actilly makes my ole eyes swim seein' the little fellers go fur me; an' ef I poke along, they'll call me back, like, an' climb me like 'possoms an' git me ter tell yarns. I haint got the spunk in me to refuse, like I would if they was bigger. Many's the comfortable time I've had a laughin' an' yarn spinin' with some urchin on my knee, ef I do say it; an' seein' yer so good natered, I acknowledge it ter *you.*

LIN. I see you have a good heart, and I for one, cannot see your ugliness as plainly as you do. Where do you live, Joe ?

HUN. Me? wal, I'm a sort uv a transient chap; I dont live anywheres. I'm stoppin' though, hereabouts this many a year; but game's gittin' skace an' I'm goin' down inter ole Kentuck, whar I kin find varmints thicker at the foot uv the Varginy mountains. Good bye boy, you've larnt me a lesson ef I am the oldest. You're the last two legged game without feathers I shall ever snap at, 'less 'tis a traitor. Here's my clinchin' bones. Yer think I'd a shot yer? Wal I would at fust, but 'fore I got done aimin', the ole kill devil wus mor'n four foot wide yer carcass. 'Scuse this brine, I'm on'y sweatin'.   [*Going, wiping his eyes*]

LIN.   Hold! What's your hurry ?

Come, you're tired, hungry. Enjoy with me
This frugal meal, my friend and let us bury
Strangeness and be friends. I'm from Kentucky.

Hun. Are ye? Wal, yer paw on that. I'm off
Take care yerself boy. [*Going.*] Hey thar! I for-
got. What's yer name?

Lin. Abram Lincoln.

Hun. Abraham Lincoln! That's a philoserphy
name, an' he's a philoserphy chap, that, kind uv
winnin' like. I had hard scratchin' to break away
from 'im. I haint the feller to eat his grub arter
I'd been plunkin' a hole through 'im. That 'ud be
heathenish. Ef ever he gits inter a scrape, an' I
hear on't, yer'll see me stick up for 'im like a she
bear. He's got a soul in 'im that's bigger'n a pung-
kin.   [*Exit* Joe.]

Lin.   Simple scene!
We have unearthed a diamond! The sensitive,
Rough man possess'd a heart too keen and soft
For undevelop'd reason. 'Tis too hard!
The mind is sometimes held in check and stayed
A lifetime from its proper course; forbidden
To expand and use its latent forces
In conqu'ring the will, 'gainst which it knowingly
Contends. How can the mind without a teacher
Essay to rule the heart? 'Twas born within
Us; tender and sensitive, with attributes,
Branches, from which emotions spring; subject
To being moulded by this mind. When in
The school of life, branches of bad intent
Are lopp'd and those of good develop'd. 'Tis thus
An infant in its mother's guiding rule
First feels, as 'twere the sunshine purity
Of a stronger, directly on the heart;
Grafting the scions in't that afterwards
Produce delicious fruitage and divine.

Mind, too new t' admit the rays of reason,
Remains uninfluenced and undevelop'd.
Reason was not born — only the instrument
On which it plays — and like the varying cadence
Of the violin, its tones are wild,
Discordant, sublimely sweet, depending
On the manner of the execution;
And like the viol, the more 'tis exercised
The more neglected, the finer or the
Harsher are its strains. 'Tis first another
Who plays upon this instrument; and then
The opening life of its possessor;
And I do feel like pitying the man
Whose heart is taught in error; whose reason
Unsophisticated, mocks, punctures, stabs
The bleeding weeping heart.

[*Works.*

'Twas a droll remark I made; "Our spotless
Yankee Nation," Well, yes; unstained she seems
And yet, like nebulæ upon the sun
She has her spots — unfit comparison —
A coalbed—peatbog better illustrate:
Years long elapsed, some loose adventurer
Thinking to profit by the circumstance,
Placed burning fagots in a gaping crevice
Of the bed, which roared and flamed unquench'd.
Perhaps the mineral seeker reaped a good profit
By this artifice; but going, failed to stanch
The hissing element that now, like crawling
Serpent, his length insinuating, descends
Deep into grottoes of the mountain, fed
From invisible aliment, establishing
Itself within its sultry den, defies
The feeble energies of man unhelp'd,
To check it. Lapping and smudging, now
Almost assuaged for want of its supporter,

Its fires for months are thought extinguished.
Anon, some overhanging, carbonaceous
Column, or cliff, its crystals disintegrated,
Tumbles. Afresh the flames are lighted; and
The monster's hideous heats and thunders dull
Produce a shock that's felt for many a mile;
And men are frightened at the phenomenon,
Perceiving that vegetation sickens;
And e'en the little birds and quadrupeds
And all that make existence cheerful, die
Or withdraw their company and leave a
Sullen and vindictive desolation!
For never shall those flames be quenched until
Th' alarmed people, into th' issuing
Crater, or ruptured culmination, with
Engines huge, shall turn a river; force an
Inundation; soak the very tissues
Shallow and deep, centre and margin through.
       This illustrates
The sin that stains my country—the wretched
Taint of slavery. The men who introduced
And cherished its infant growth have vanish'd.
Through the propensity of man to sneer
At labor, the service of poor, unpaid,
Degraded slaves, was forced, to till the plump,
Alluvial acres of our southern realm;
First in small parcels, till the fatten'd lords,
Proud and haughty, despising manual toil,
Began to cast about for means to stock
More plentifully, with these poor bondsmen,
Their increasing tillage. The slave trade not
Yielding the supply, recourse was had to
Breeding. 'Twas thus the loathesome pestilence
Of slavery inhumanly began its
Ghastly inculcations; and the desire
In all of Afric's race for freer lives

And culture, make the freedom of free men,
Free conversation, free, frank, ingenuousness,
Free, loving confidence, free schools, free work,
Yes, all that marks enlightened happiness,
With them, most incompatible!   Where'er
The lurking wrong, you'll find a dagger to
Defend it.   Whate'er that wrong, 'tis hidden.
Thus habit shields the crime; for slavecraft's clutch'd
By th' autocrat whose class law power, on his
Plantation, reigns supreme.   He pompous grows,
And insolent; and like a tyrant, gluts
His own passions in licensed lust and blood;
And men of other countries and other
Views, when passing his domain, must warn the
Tempted tongue.   Oh, my dear country!   When will
The crater open that floods may enter
And annihilate thy wrongs?   Could I, by
Adding knowledge and polish to my small
Accomplishments, do aught to mitigate,
Or stay the deadly doom which I perceive
Foreshadowed in this curse: stop th' impending
Tempest; reconcile the lurking spirit
Of hate, swift widening 'twixt North and South.—
Could I contribute t' avert the mischief,
I'd sacrifice my time, my pains, my life,
     In such a goodly business.

THE GREAT REBELLION.

DRAMATIS PERSONÆ.

LINCOLN, the Rail-splitter; afterwards President.
SEWARD, Secretary to LINCOLN.
JOE, a hunter; lost brother to FLORENCE.
JOHN BROWN, a raider and martyr.
COP, a rebel sympathizer.
DAVIS, President of the Confederacy.
STEVENS, Vice President of Confederacy.

LEE,
BEAUREGARD, } Generals of Confederate armies.

BRECKINRIDGE,
WIGFALL,
TOOMBS, } Secretaries to DAVIS.
FLOYD,

MASON,
SLIDELL, } Envoys plenipotentiary

MEAD,
REYNOLDS, } Generals in the Union armies.
CUSTER,

TAYLOR, a Union colonel.
QUASHY, negro carpenter; afterwards a runaway.

WINDER,
TURNER, } keepers of Confederate prisons.
WIRTZ,

BOB, a Union volunteer.
HARMON, a rebel sympathizer.
BILL, a rummy and office holder.

MARY, wife to LINCOLN.
ADELINA, Wife to SEWARD.
FLORENCE, nurse and espion; sister to JOE.
MRS. DAVIS, wife to the dictator.

Soldiers, Surgeons, Pickets, Sharp-shooters, Hangman, Messengers, Masters, Slaves, Citizens, a Sheriff, Civilians, a Sergeant and attendants.

THE GREAT REBELLION.

ACT I.

SCENE I. *A Street in Harper's Ferry.*

Enter CITIZENS *in confusion.*

First CIT. Hello! What's the excitement?

Second CIT. Excitement! You're slow at news. The town has been attacked by robbers!

First CIT. By robbers! Impossible, I'm amazed! Say, neighbor, what's your hurry? You've But one life to live. If that's the way you Live it though, you'll find it short.

Sec. CIT. Don't hinder me. The length of my life depends upon the activity of my legs. Hinder me not, I say. D'ye think I'm going to tarry in this hornet's nest while the yaller jackets are making such free use of their gaffs?

First CIT. What's up?

Third CIT. Enough. The town is overrun with abolitionists. There's more'n a thousand. They're running off the niggers by the dozen. They've got a reg'lar gineral; a savage abolitionist big enough to eat any two common sized niggers at a meal. They've driven the soldiers out of the town, and the people are leaving in great haste for safety. I expect we'll all be killed. [*Exit.*

First CIT. This must be all excitement. I'll look to't.

It is the wild st folly to suppose
That men would organize, with leaders, and
March in armies to emancipate the slaves.
Directly against the Constitution
Of the government and statutes of the
States.　I own that slavery, as conducted,
(And 'tis a goading crime 'gainst God and man)
Has, by its encroachments, wrought jealousies
And distrusts amongst the people, to such
Harsh degree that lawyers, statesmen, solid
Farmers and men of traffic unite in
Grave discussion, dispensing theories,
While others clamor with unrestrain'd
Vehemence the justice or injustice
Of the cause.　I'll scan this raid.　[*Exeunt omnes.*

SCENE II.　*Idem.　A roadside by the river.*
Enter two SLAVES.

First SLAVE.　Say, Sambo, git behine dis yer
woodpile.　I's afeer'd!

Second SLAVE.　Wot yo 'feer'd 'bout, Quash?
D'ye 'strust de good Lawd?　I's full ob jubilation?

Enter several SLAVES.

Third SLAVE.　De Lor' be praised!　De 'lishun-
ists is come.　De Lor' be praised.　We know dar'd
come anuder Moses fur to lead us out o' bondage
into de land ob Canaan, jes like de Isrilites was.

First SLAVE.　Stop dat shoutin' dar, niggah.　Be
quiet, yu'll git foun' out.　Gorry!　If ole Mars come
'long h'yer he'll warm yer ole black hide wif suffin'
wus'n de kintessence ob kyan pepper.　Don' yeu
try dat hollerin' on agin'!

Fourth SLAVE.　Gemlem, I's ob de same 'pinyin
wi' Jambo; but shorely, de good Moses is come
wif a whole army.　I seed 'im wan 'ee cum dis yer
bressed mornin'.　'Ee wont hab to take us dis time
cross de Red Sea; on'y but jes de 'Tomac; an' dar

we kin git 'board ob de undergroun' railroad an'
migrate wid de welocity ob de telegraph wires an'
wid our darlin' chillun' wid us, we'll go jicin' ober
de prospec' 'bout our 'rac'lous 'scape out from de
land ob Egyp'.

Fifth SLAVE. I'se bin callatin' on dis'ere dis good
wile. Ole mars cut stick an' run an' a'most ebery
body else 'cept us niggas, hea, hea, hea, I tinks
we'll be apt to run too—todder d'rection, yah! He,
hea, hea. [*Sings*]
I heard de trumpet sounding, sounding, sounding,
I heard de trumpet sounding on dat great day.
  ALL. 'Tis de hand ob de Lawd is o'er us
    Though clouds do rise before us,
    To Canaan He'll restore us
An' we'll soun' de jubilee.
Fifth SLAVE. Our bonds shall soon be broken,
  broken, broken,
Our bonds will all be broken on dat glad day
ALL. When dis poor down-trodden nation
    Oh African relation,
    Wi' de free shall take dere station,
Den we'll soun' de jubilee.
      Enter MASTER *with a whip.*

MAS. Wow, now, here you are; you confounded pack! I thought you had run off with that infernal ab—hem—robber. I mean. What are you
making all this powwow about?

First SLAVE. Oh, good mars, we's ter'ble frightened at de robbers; an' 'liberatin' 'bout—

MAS. I'll deliberate you, you swarthy froth from
bedlam! Go home and go to work! The vandals
are arrested and shall hang. Take that, and that,
and that, and that for disobedience. Now hustle,
or by Heavens! I'll have you all hanged—every
black effigy of Satan. [*Exeunt omnes.*

SCENE III. *A cell in a prison.*

Enter KEEPER. *with keys.*

KEEP. 'Tis strange that such brusque things
    should come to pass.
The man looks fine, of noble bearing; grac'd,
So far as one should fathom, with pungent sense.
A man endow'd with lordly bearing; power
Of wielding sway ; or girding great actions ; the
Energy possessing, of a lion,   [*Knocking outside.*
The meekness of a lamb.   Ho, who comes there ?

   VISITOR. Is this the place where John Brown's
    imprisoned ?

   KEEP. Yes, stand back; none can enter. I'm under
Special orders from the Governor to
Admit no man.

   VIS. I pray you, hear my plea. He is a friend;
An old acquaintance ; besides ; I have these
Certificates and notes of introduction
From gentlemen of bearing in the realm ;
Proof of my loyalty and safe intent.

   KEEP. [*Reads.*]   Well, come in ;

Enter VISITOR,

But clip it ; make short the colloquy.   A
Bench Sir. I'll go bring him. How sound reports?
How look the people on this high treason ?
Do they sanction it ?

   VIS. Far from it. Excitement foams too high for
Solid judgment. But if from both idle and
Candid converse of the million we take
Parts, weigh them. analyze the compound or their
Bulk compare, we'll have more sympathy than
Anger; more thought than pugnacity; more
Feeling than vindictiveness. Indisposed
To quarrel, yet ready for the onset,
We're a'tiptoe, sir; in mazy quivers.

The world's agog—in hesitancy 'twixt two
Decisions. Not that there lies i'the madden'd
Mob no coefficient of cank'ring hate
And scowling jealousy. Our sin has wax'd
National and become common. The slave
Growl, go where you may, is coupled with this
John Brown negro raid; and some proclaim his
Treason as the sure harbinger of war.
The South's exasperated at the North's
Encroachments, the North's exasperated
At the South's encroachments! Good men tremble
Lest words turn to blows.

Enter John Brown *from his cell, led by keeper.*

J. B. Ho, good comrade, how art thou? I'm glad
Thou'st come. Take my letters and accoutrements
In charge; and I do commission thee
As well, to bear my blessing to my household.

Vis. Ah, my old friend; your words ring o-
minous.
I cannot realize—

J. B. Stop. Thy sighs are useless and uncalled
for. *[Exit* Keeper.
Shed not a tear for me; for if I can afford
To lose myself, thou canst afford to lose me.
The lawful penalty of my offense
Is death. 'Tis frivolous whining to condole
Or grieve. The tyrant, to perpetuate
His devil work, compounds iniquity
Into law. I've laid my life an off'ring
To rupture both the evil and its fell
Offspring, the law. I'm willing then, to grope
These cobwebb'd lairs, and snuff miasma, and
More, to save my fellow—aye, even to
Leap the breakneck—'Tis the curse must perish;
The curse of slavery, the noxious blight

That shrouds humanity; shames manhood and
Makes of liberty a chattering coward.
It is not that I wish to be avenged
Because my sons were slain; God will avenge,
Them. On such power and wisdom I rely.
Tell me not, then, of rights in human toads
To hold their kin in bonds. There's my master.
Him I'm serving. Him alone, obeying;
As common guide to virtue for all men.
We hold all mankind created equal;
Whether in simple childhood, in manhood
Or old age, nation, sex or color. Here
Is their birthright—the Book of the Almighty
And the Constitution! My punishment
Is death. Well, I forgive the henchman. If
The black nightcap's mirk do awe the thoughtbound,
If, through my doom men's souls are convicted
Of slavery's evil; if, in my dying,
Men's minds be enlighten'd to slavery's evil;
If, by my dying, humanity be
Wak'd 'gainst slavery's evil, then, welcome death!
His sting is impotent; and I, most rich,
In payment of this sacrifice, shall mount
The glutton gallows, with hopes as buoyant
As an infant's pulse; and in a manly
Death, will rend the tyrant's chains. Men clamor
For my blood. They've forged these laws; I suffer
Them; though they smudge as dark and infamous
As the clammy fog that cases in the
Nucleus of hell! Oh, may these murder'd
Bones ne'er sleep; but haunt in horrid winding
Sheets, with og'rish mock, their dormitories;
And devils flap their webb'd and moping pennants
Round, o'er orgies demoniacal yelling;
Till jaded conscience, South, and ripen'd
Forces, North, conspire to crush these wrongs.

Re-enter KEEPER *with* SHERIFF *and* OFFICERS,

SHERIFF. Your time is come,
Good friend. The law respectfully fore-knells
That we do interrupt this colloquy.
The hour is swift approaching to your end.
Shall I admit a chaplain?

J. B. Of holy counsellors have I no need,
Save One. Dispatch this business quietly
And quickly.

*Sheriff advances. Marshall administers the man-
acles. Officers take their stand on each side of prisoner, and march toward the gallows. Exeunt omnes.*

SCENE IV. *A gallows on the green.*

Enter HANGMAN *and Negro* CARPENTER.

HANG. Dees ees vun contrée veree pecoolaire, I
teenks. Vun co-oop an' ze ozer down.

CARP. I does'nt zac'ly un'stan' de meanin' ob
dat obsarvation, sah. Please 'splain your position.

HANG. Mon Dieu! Zat ees peek talk fur to
come from under wool. Vat you say?

CARP. I say, I dont ccmprehen' wot *you* say.

HANG. Ver' vell, I say vun ko down an' same
time his voisin he ko oop, eh? You ought to guess
zat moosh vizout scratchin'. Look'ee now yoo see
vun gallus zaire?

CARP. I ought to know suffin' consarnin' dat.
I's de chile wot got up dat ar histin'-jack, sah.

HANG. Ver' vell, I say ven vun ko oop, ze uzer he
come down; comprenez? Dees Jean Brown, vous
l' appelez, ees vun square martyre for all of ze wool-
ly-heads. Ver' vell, now, je suppose zat ce martyre
au ransom for all dees wool, git him neck in von
mauvais piége, and git zat leetle cord, pliée in vun
slipknot; savez-vous? And some pauvre diable
as me he shall have ze quoi à manger for zat service,

he cut cette cord là, savez, zat hold ze grand ballance; allez! Alors, ze vun he monte oop, and vun he tombe down, n'est pas? Eh bien, je dis zees contrée he got d'institutions pecooliares.

CARP. Wot yo gwang to do wid yer lor breakers in yer own kentry fur de high crime ob treason, sah?

HANG. Va, ve cuts ze heads off, allez; tout simplement. No saire, yoo'll see no oops an' downs, là bas! Ze offizaire of ze law, he not villin' to help ze poor man oop. If he be born oop, he stay oop; if he be born down, ver vell, he stay down; mais, mon dieu, je trouve zat in yoor bonne contrée he git help oop, bien souvant, on top of vun leetle gallus, allez; an' ze nobler teengs vat he do, ze higher he git lifted an' ze leetler big teengs vat he steal he git let down easy; voyez vous, zat in votre bonne contrée to git put down c'est to be lift up; vite, allez! Zat ees pourquoi que je dis cette contrée he got d'institutions particulières. Comprenez?

CARP. Lor' wot mul'tudes ob folks is come to see dis ex'cution!

Enter SHERIFF *with officers and guard;* JOHN BROWN *and* VISITOR *between them. Weeping friends and a multitude following. Group of negroes shying about, at a distance.*

VIS. Oh my dear friend....

J. B. My name's John Brown.

VIS. Nay, do not rebuke me; this is a gloomy hour.

J. B. 'Twill soon be past. Be faithful to thy charge.
Bear my will and letters to my household.
Shake hands with each and say that father lov'd,
And commended them to the Great Father
And died happy.

Brown *mounts the scaffold and Sheriff administers the slip-knot and black cap. Mixed sobs and jeers heard.*

Sher. Five minutes time are given you to confess
Or give directions for your effects....

J. B. Avaunt, ye maudlin pand'rers of the law!
Am I one who basely dies, driveling
Confessions which compromise God's mandate?
Nor do I quake in simp'ring negligence
Of thine and mine. Commit this tragedy
Betimes. I'm ready.

Executioner *draws and curtain falls. Moans and jeers swell louder from the stage.*

Scene V. *A graveyard by moonlight.*
Enter a numerous band of Slaves, singing.

QUARTETTE.

De mornin' star ob freedom rises o'er de eastern sky
An' de tyrants wi' de swords an' raids ob champions
shall die,
Though ole John Brown an' comrades in dar
graves low lie
Dar souls, dey're marchin' on.

ALL.

Glory, glory, Hallelujah!
Glory, glory, Hallelujah!
Glory, glory, Hallelujah!
Dar souls are marchin' on.

QUARTETTE.

Dey're fannin' to de flames freedom's dross consum-
in' fires,
Dey're livenin' de hearts ob men wi' nobler desires,
For to battle wid oppression dar army never tires
As dar souls go marchin' on.

ALL.

We see de t'rones a shakin' afore dar mighty tread
An' de man drivin' despotis' a tremblin' wi' dread,
An' a hollerin' for de big moguls to kiver up
    its head
As dey go marchin' on.

ALL.

Glory, glory, Hallelujah!
Glory, glory, Hallelujah!
Glory, glory, Hallelujah!
Dar souls are marchin' on.

QUARTETTE.

We see de people risin' up an' offerin' dar han's
To all ob de Brudderen in all norvern lan's,
An' Dixie's line'll disappear like tracks in
    hurricanes
As dar souls go marchin' on.

ALL.

Glory, glory, Hallelujah!
Glory, glory, Hallelujah!
Glory, glory, Hallelujah!
Dar souls are marchin' on.

ACT II.

Enter Jefferson Davis.

DAVIS. THE HOUR of midnight's come. High
    time it is,
The banded knights of this conclavium
Be noislessly approaching. The mighty
Business of disunion! Complete o'erthrow
Of this inchoate creature—the Republic.
Our "Institution" leans for its bold life
Upon such action! Union and slavery
Are discrepant sisters. The Union is
Too free. A lash and auction-thong are tools
Befitting best the slave. They liven and
Make keen his brawn; and that suffices for
The master's ends. A narrow mind has not
Enough of thwack to keep the limbs astir.
Brains may supply Caucasians with a forte
Which quickens muscle and shapes ambition,
Whose constant rub creates a fev'rish heat
And renders inaction painful. Here's a
Secret of the growing strength of northern
Enterprise. But the numb slave, possessing
Vig'rous phisique and low front, wants, like the
Ox, the pungent suasion of a lash, to
Quicken his inertia; make him useful.

T'will never do to teach him, or waken
The dim ray of mental force he gathers.
Nay, one must urge branal stupidity;
Deny him brain developments; consign
His gift of thought to Lollards' pyre-stake.
We'll cultivate by scientific mix
The best corporeal status of the race.
Egad! The air's too free for slavery.
One of the two must go. Ah liberty,
Thou'rt meek and childish; thou hast no masters;
Control'st thyself, eh; credulous myops!
Forgiving, canst not judge an enemy
Till thou feel'st his cut; and yet a Ceasar,
That coys arms and sympathies and fellows!
I'll be thy Brutus; yet unlike a Brutus,
Will erect a throne and mount its sella.
An Anglo-Columbian monarchy
On bondage basis! Northmen, forever
Hush your brawl of vapid Monroe doctrines.
Shrewd kingdoms of the earth shall recognize

    Enter LEE, MASON, SLIDELL, WISE, BEAURE-
GARD, RHETT, WIGFALL, TOOMBS, FLOYD *and others.*

And uphold *me.* Ho, friends, good morrow,
How fare you? Are the rest forthcoming? Past
Is the midnight and I'm getting nervous.
Welcome, most welcome, gentlemen. We're bound
By previous oath most sacred, to keep our
Councils secret. Now whilst the clouds of war
Are bursting, must we refresh this promise;
Even tho' we scribe our names with crayons ting'd
In blood; must close these talks hebdomadal
This night, that we best hasten to the front
And quit this stifling city, putrid of
Saucy thoughts which smut the age. The oath is
Secresy, fidelity and resolve.

Momentous launch; the outcomings whereof
Depend upon your energies.   I call
This Club to order.   Brethren step forward.
It behoves us then, t' renew our oath
This night.   Mason, to your experience
And statesmanship I do trust this solemn
Work.   Sagacity is a green palmetto
From whose branches hangs concealed a whipcord.
This night we grasp our lives in hand, to shape
The deeds which tremblingly do darkle 'neath
The sword of Damocles.

    MASON.   The bells have toll'd the om'nous hour
    of twelve.
A flitting moment gone, and all was peace.
The haughty north with her proud millions, sleeps
The world's slumbers.   Yet methinks a nightmare
Broods o'er her dormant thought; some startling
Premonitor to brawl mysterious rumor
Of the presence of the skinny monster,

    Enter STEVENS, *unobserved.*

War, that with the peal of yonder midnight
Bell, was born.   The great election's o'er.   At last
The slurring mudsills have their president!
Regret it not.   Many long years has good
King Cotton ruled and chafed the yapping north
With lion's warning to beware trespass
On his fav'rite mess.   All those sullen years
That grease smear'd north, like curling curs obey'd.
The southern lion, having waxed careless
And incautious of the harmless spaniel,
Snapping at his heels, o'erlooked th' encroachment.
At length arousing, he this night, bursts forth
In self vindication, with deaf'ning roar
And the dumb enemy shall be devoured.
The nature of our Slave Institution
Is retrogade.   She beckons backward to

The sunny days of feudal Europe; when
Title'd lords, in equipage august, with
Liveried retinue, from palace, castle,
Or green bower proceeded, each with his train
Of beaut'ous belles, array'd in rarest silks
And garlanded with aromatic flowers
And spark'ling diamonds, to join the thrilling
Chase, and with many a recreant pastime
While the languid hour.   She beckons backward
To the golden days of chivalry; when
Strong men asserted manhood.   When handsome
Knights, and bold, lent their protection to the
Fair.   When gilded kings, on thrones of burnish'd
Gold, held pompous parlance with the mighty.
When lords and courtiers and sweet ladies, all,
Studied but to be happy.   Him born of
Royal parentage, all worshipp'd; him born
Of noble, all honored; but he, whòse lot
It was t' inherit rags—Bah I've no time
To fritter in huts of poverty; vile
And unlettered were they; yet then, as now,
Made good tillers of the soil; good drudges,
Good soldiers; and when kept ignorant of
Their combin'd strength, were most invaluable.
Glance, ye men of blood, upon those genial
Ages of the past.   Those days of sunny
Pleasure that drifted, wafted the passive
Lives of men on balmy zephyrs and tipped
Th' intoxicating cup of happiness,
Sweet happiness, royal and sparkling!   And
Then, reflect that ye claim geniture, through
Lineage direct, of noble blood.
Reflect that your prerogative and claim
On lands transmitted to your kin by kings,
Are curtailed and contested by yankee
Innovation; by the loquacious

Yankee; the meddlesome yankee; th' obtrusive
Ubiquitous, oppugnant yankee!   He
Cannot file a claim to noble blood, sprung
As he is from banish'd convict cion,
So seeks, by taking vantage of new lands
I'the new found world whereon he squats and draws
A squeaking file, a noisy sledge, making
The din of Vulcan's thunder mountain with
Greasy thews and rattling pate, t' institute
Reforms; base governments on theories
Of equal rights, that lift the sluggish slaves
As high as ye ; and jabbers a jargon
Never quell'd 'gainst your acknowledg'd right to
Hold them bondsmen.   Ye men of blood, reflect.
Reflect upon the outrages ye smart
And answer me.   Will ye endure it?

    ALL.   [*except Stevens*]   No.
    MAS.   Will ye resist it?
    ALL.   We will, we will.
    MAS.   Will ye dislodge th' usurping mountebank
And on his quitted claim, build the sacred
Empire of your inheritance?
    ALL.   We will. So help us God!
    MAS.   Then, ere ye mount the project, take oath;
Each speaking loud his name where I use mine.

    All, [*except Stevens, who is unnoticed*] *form a ring
each touching the book.*

I, John Mason, most solemnly do swear
That from this hour I will devote my strength,
My will, my influence, my property,
Even my life will sacrifice, in the
Intent and purpose of destroying northern
Liberties, crushing democracy by
Arm'd rebellion and for the purpose of
Creating, of the Southern States, and as
Much of the North as in our hands shall fall.

An empire, on the slave basis. For this,
I will wage war upon the feudal, and
Ennobling principal that might makes right;
Holding all enemies as deadly foes
Deserving death by torture; and I will
Not discriminate 'twixt age or sex, rich or
Poor, civil or military; but strike
Vengeance on the heads of all within my
Grasp, entombing them in loathsome prison
Caves, or hurrying them to block and vale and
Scaffold to meet an unrepentant doom;
And further; as in feudal ages, I
Will hold hostages, abnegate pardons,
Wreak retaliation, practice civil
Espionage and keep hir'd assassins.
To do these deeds infernal do I swear,
—The moral ethics of wars in ages
Mediœval, and of antiquity,
My justifiers—till my enemies
Are overwhelmed, subjugated or
Destroyed; and in the virtue of this oath
Do I inaugurate, proclaim, and launch
Upon the blasts, a war, extirpating
The northern principles. So help me God.

WIGFALL. Mr. chairman. It is now first in the
order of business, and as the power rests upon the
decision of this body, exclusively, let us attend to
the appointment of rulers and to the denomination
of our inchoate confederacy.

SLIDELL. The suggestion of the Hon. Senator, is
most appropriate. The South is expected to adopt
an ordinance of secession. Measures have already
been taken to frame these ordinances, and immediately pass them through the several legislative councils of the state; and that this important feature of
our strategy may not fail, paid emissaries have been

sent to canvass each state and inflame the minds
of the populace in our favor. But immediately the
States secede, they become a disorganized mass,
unless they resolve themselves into a government,
with name and head.

DAVIS. One of the worthy personages present
must be chosen Dictator and commander in chief.
Gentlemen whom will you have ?

RHETT. No one would seem more capable to en-
gineer, as civil head and chief of military, than our
worthy chairman, whom I nominate.

DAVIS. Gentlemen, I beg you to excuse me.
The noble gentleman himself, methinks,
Were better fitted for that office ; or
The worthy senator from Georgia.

TOOMBS. Mr Chairman, two or three gentlemen
are nominated. I move the president be elected
by ballot of the club.

WIGF. Allow me to second this proposition.

DAVIS. Gentlemen. It is both proposed and
seconded, that a President, Commander in chief or
Dictator, whose duty it shall be to arrange and conduct the important business of this Confederation,
be chosen from the three nominated. Are you
ready for the question?

ALL. Ready.

DAVIS. All ye who favor this movement, signify by an uplifted hand. Down. Contrary by same
sign. Carried. Bring out the ballot box.
Good friends, consider well before you choose ;
Much doth depend upon the wisdom of
This cast. [*Each puts his slip of paper into the
box.*

HERALD. [*To* DAVIS.] I do declare your worth-
iness elected.

WIGF. I move, Mr. Chairman, that this territo-

ry over which you are chosen to preside, receive,
pro tempore, the appellation of the Confederate
States.

TOOMBS. I second the motion.

DAVIS. It is motioned and seconded that the
territory over which you have called me to preside
shall be known as the Confederate States of America, until we gain our independence. All who
favor that, signify their approval by the good
word, I. Unanimous! A toast for the Southern Confederacy. [*Shouting and cheering.*]
Robert E. Lee, I appoint you Lieutenant General.
Commander of my forces in Northern Virginia.
I shall eventually make you ruler over my
Maryland.

STEPH. [*Aside.*] My Maryland; mark, *my*
Maryland!

DAVIS. As the town of Washington is situated
within the [*Ghost, observed only by* STEVENS, *is seen
writing each name upon the wall in large blood letters.*]
geographical limits of My Maryland, and as it, like
dumb creatures, will probably make some slight
resistance, I shall send you with a good force and
with directions to capture it within three months.
G. T Beauregard, sir, I make you Major General
and shall give you a command duly. Messrs, Mason and Slidell, I appoint you straightway, ministers
plenepotentiary to England and France; and your
eminent qualifications as diplomatists, sanction my
decision. Leave no strategy untried, but forthwith
effect a recognition of my Confederacy.

STEPH. [*Aside.*] My Confederacy! Too me-
chanical. The thing is cut and dried.

DAVIS. Behold, now from this seat too common, we
Descend, that we ascend the throne of a

New born principality!   But lest ye
Marvel, or think these words too bold, 'tis not
A throne veritable we do mount, but
A gigantic power in embryo ; composed
Of parts, dissevered by dissentions, strong
In union and wanting but organic
Joint through tact of leadership.   By your shrewd
Judgment and assistance in the work of
War and of coördination, we do
Promise to develop, of this strugg'ling,
Prone constituency, an empire so grand,
So mighty, so imposing, that e'en the
Spirits of Zingis Khan, and Mahmoud shall
See their hopes eclipsed.   Let us dissolve these
Gatherings nocturnal and henceforth act
Before the open world.   Let wine be brought,
That each may drink the others' health and ray
The nightly shadows.

   STEPH. [*Aside.*] My Maryland, *My* Confederacy!
By Jove, I cannot brook it!   'Tis too strong.   [*To*
DAVIS].   'Whom the gods would destroy, they
   first make mad.'
O, vir miserrime !   Quae vident oculi ?
These are the orgies saturnalian;
Our gift from Pluto.   I did think the god
Of drunkenness, abashed and stupefied
O'er scenes, eclipsing the damning revels
Of degen'rate Rome, would scarce introduce
The demon bowl on such a night as this !
Spite of all the murky struggles of my
Repellant soul, after the dismal deeds ·
Of this portentious night, this mawkish night;
Whose consequence shall go far to fabric
History ; whose typified events shall
Be inscribed in blood but ne'er the half be
Chronicled, behold the bacchanal !   Tell

Me, infatuate revelers, tell me,
Do ye dare ween that all these secret schemes,
Revolting plots and bandit oaths, o'erglozed
To feasibility b'inciting wine,
Lascivious dance, and croaky cheering,
Make your mad treason less like Catiline's.
I warn ye of your madness. Beware how
Ye foment the powder of contending
Elements—slav'ry and freedom. Inborn,
Their nature is antagonistical
As heaven and hell; and though by preference
I espouse the cause of slav'ry, yet I
Tremble lest too soon they come to deadly
Tilt. Sir, 'twill not be a re-enactment
Of Neronian scenes; tyrants have but the
Sultry passions of their depravity
To urge a brutal carnage. Nor will it
Be a glum rehash of deeds Caligulan,
Where vagrant wrath let carmine waters paint
The channel of classic Tiber with tint
From veins of innocence; whose fountain head
The reeking knife and axe; whose name was death.
Nay, 'twill be a shock electrical from
Batteries surcharg'd like long pent lightnings,
From that more dang'rous urgent, a people's
Will!   Will ye thus aggravate the friction
Of contumacy, of sneer, of censure,
Rasping our smarting sores, with twit, snub, jeer?
This rub has charged both batt'ries to bursting.
Factions are wrecking candor, drifting to
Madness; fretting with ideas, principles
Of which they have not brain to work a clear
Solution.   The hairbrain'd North, too hot for
Sane reflections, catch the intelligence
Of our faults which flit the wires; and wanting
Charity and sense, proclaim with frothing

Mouths, bellowing throats,and frantic gesture
Their wild exaggerations, forcing a
Bias throughout the land against us; whilst we,
Too sensitive, and wanting prudence, fall
Back upon the old ancestral warfare;
Forgetting that law and order are the
Fruit of judgment.   We burn t'assail and
Punish with a reckless hand.   We foster
Unchristian thoughts; harbor sullen hatreds;
Bosom   implacability, chronic
With gangrene of a fire-fed lust for blood
And glory; and thus fan follies' foibles.
Passions, Sir,   Wilt thou the hell-blasts hotter?
Spare me the grim responsibility
Of medium through whom these lightnings fork'd
Shall burst their bounds!   'Twere a rencounter
Whose rams of war must jar both heaven and
Earth.   A swoop that in fierce grapple hawks hosts
Who fight not for a master, but for a
Principle.   Green in each warrior's breast.
Og'rish and mad, do I foresee this jam.
Children made homeless, and homes heartless;
        waste
And desolation; cold blooded butcheries;
Annihilating battles; brute impulse
Infuriated; the weepings of woe
Mock'd by the lechery of unpent sin;
Wealth bankrupt; treasuries depleted;
Laws nullified; society awreck;
Morals aswoon; religion banished....
    DAVIS.   Hold, hold, good friend!   Thy elegy
Ports terror.   Thou shockst us.   Prithee prorogue
Yon thrilling figure.   The company are
Siezed with   pangs of   conscience and   crouch
        trembling.
Didst thus speedily disclaim thine oath?

STEPH.   Tell me not of that oath.   Did I begore
This hand or black this heart with idle oaths?
I tarried contemplating the
The doings of a sprite that stalked the room
With real presence, or was bred of my
Imagination, and scrawled with blood red
Letters the new Belshazzar's doom.
    DAVIS.   Friends, did you see a spirit?
    TOOMBS.   We saw none.
    SLI.   'Twas all a picture of a fervid brain.
    WIGF.   I fear this augurs badly for our cause;
What uncouth marks are those?
    STEPH.   Work of that ghostly hand.
    MAS.   Nonsense, nonsense.   Take down that
        bloody scrawl.
There's a traitor present.
    BEAU.   Let him be caught and like a traitor die.
    LEE.   Friends banish this causeless, terror ere it
Become a precedent.   If we set out
Upon this enterprise whilst gaunt omens
Rack us, the same dejection will teaze till
Doomsday.   You're niggling with forebodings.
It's a good general that outgenerals
Gloom.   Away with it.   Let work and mirth go
Hand in hand.   Here, Aleck, take a glass.
    DAV.   Good friend, 'tis now too late to moralize.
This quarrel is foregone.   Eloquence and
Caution craze one's talk of things unlikely.
We play prophetic language, hinting at
Dangers, yet a blind incredulous can
See in ours a brilliant undertaking.
We speak of media that must conduct
With murderous onset th' impassioned
Bolts of war; yet cannot meet arguments
Thrice dead!   Has not the Northerners' election
Declared hostilities?   Will ye tamely

Cower to that gaunt hoosier whom for want of
Better stock, they've chosen tyrant?   A tann'd
Faced rail-splitter!   A beast untam'd, as the
Owl-denn'd prairies, whence he hails.
    Steph.   Dont call Abe Lincoln either beast
      or fool.
    Mas.   Hold, stop this senseless jangle.   It
      breeds ill.
    Lee.   Come, Aleck, you have not yet accepted
      our toast.
    Wigf.   We were going to nominate you Vice
President; but an unsound friend may be a danger-
ous ally.
    Steph.   You'll not find me unsound when there's
      a shade
Of hope.   By predilection, I'm with you.
    Hunter.   You hint that you would accept this
office and be loyal, if it were offered you?
    Steph.   First I must know my honors, after the
Struggle's past and independence won.
    Davis.   Sir, long have we placed security on
Your sage counsel, and cool candor ; and now
We stand amazed at these glum bodings, which
Seem strangely urged, as though an artifice
To try us.   Say you accept our offer
And you shall be a title'd lord, grace'd with
A dukedom, embracing all the acres
Of your native state.
    Steph.   On these conditions I accept.
    Wigf.   Now, since the harmony of consent
chords with the harmony of music, let us be glad
and drink wine and toasts; with cheers for Davis
and Stephens, king and prime ministers of a new
born principality;   [*Hurrahs.*]
    Steph.   [*Aside.*] So they concluded to notice the
hunchback.   Sold!   Principle for honors.   Pre-

carious. Who runs no ventures stands no chances. Good bargain! Hem.

Scene II. *A Country Roadside.*

Enter Quashy *the Carpenter.*

Quash. Well, 'taint a good year gone sens I made poor John Brown's gallus. I promised dis yer nigger 'twould be de last 'litionist's gallus dey'd force 'im to make, an' I've kep my word at de cost ob runnin' away. Here I is, up here, norf ob Mason an' Dixie's line safe; yet I feels kinder skittish whenever I meets a white man. Dey aint zactly what I trought dey was. Some on em's bery kind, but odders is mighty sabage. I'se gin ole mars de slip, an' less some demercrat takes de wantage ob de fugertive slave laws to git de premium on my head, I guess I'll git clar dis yer time from bondage. Yah, heah, heah, yah. I feels merry ober dat an' I trusts in de Lawd. Suffin's tellin' me I shall see my poor wife and chillun agin. Dey've killed de poor ole martyr wat 'tempted to liberate us poor darkies, but anudder Moses'll spring up from his ashes, an' de poor darks'll be all set free. But stop, nig, who dat?

Enter Copperhead.

Cop. By Jove! Here comes a runaway nigger. My booty. I'll make a cool thousand on him; fat sleek and greasy; just escaped from the planter— the *poor* planter! What a *ruinous* loss! Hello nig, which way?

Quash. I'se gwine home, sah.

Cop. Where do you live?

Quash. Up on de hill, yen.

Cop. You lie sir, I'm acquainted hereabouts, and know there's no such ebony growing green on these hills. I arrest you for a runaway slave according to law.

QUASH. Stan' back Sah, dont put dem fingers on dis chile.

COP. [*Seizing him*] Help, help, I demand help in the name of the fugitive slave law!

QUASH. [*Knocking him down.*] Han's off, I, say, sah.

Enter Hunting Joe.

COP. Oh, heigh! Here, here, old fellow, lend a hand.

JOE. What you doin' with that ar nigger?

COP. I arrest him as a runaway; and I command you to help me, according to law.

JOE. Are yo a runaway, nig? Yo mought as wal own up as lie.

QUASH. [*Dropping on his knees.*] O Lor' have mercy on my poor wife an' chillun.

COP. Here, come with me. Ho, help!

JOE. Shet up that ar bellerin' yo apish booby.

COP. What's that you call me? Do you know whom you are speaking to? It so happens that I helped make the law in question.

QUASH. Oh please, mars gunner, take my part.

JOE. Go 'way from me nigger. Here, come back. Set down on the grass thar. [*To Cop.*] I say sir, you're a gen'wine, loafin' baboon. What d'ye cal'late ter do with that ar nigger wunst you've got 'im across Mason and Dixie's line?

COP. I shall advertize, and restore him to his master.

JOE. Wal, spose yo did'nt find any owner.

COP. In that case I shall dispose of him on my own terms,

JOE. Wal, I understan'; yo mean ter kidnap that ar nigger, an' send 'im inter captiverty, an' bein' a p'litical or some other swindlin' rooster yo'd stan' a fair chance, bein' as the poor feller's got no friends.

Yo take advantage of weakness an' the lobby laws, an' hits nobody but a dishonest coward'll do it.

Cop. You lantern jawed—

Joe. [*Seizing him.*] Look'ee, d'yo call hit yer place fur to call me names? Now walk, Whistle, nig, "Go you rogue you," Out, march. Halt a minute. Take off yer hat an' holler hurrah for Abe Lincoln. Here nig, dance 'im a double shuffle jes fur to make 'im feel merry. Shout I say.

Cop. Hur, hur, rah.

Joe. Louder!

Cop. Why dont you order me to shoot myself? I'd rather do it. It's against my principles to hurrah for old Abe.

Joe. Time enough ter shute yerself arterwards if ye've got the grit. I own yo need shutin' but its too good fur ye now. The devil haint got a hole hot enough yit, fur ter stow away yer carcass. Yell now, yo cowardly nigger-thief, louder, louder, I say.

Cop. Hurrah for Abe Lincoln.

Joe. Thar, now, nig, whistle; an' yo nigger butcher, march under my safe conduct, Forward, march! [*Exeunt* Joe *and* Cop, *the former having him by the collar.*]

Quash. Oh, I'se free! I'se 'scaped! Blessins 'pon dat long legged, gunnin' man, wid de skin breeches! Yah, I'se happy now; but I blebe ef I'd a chonked once I'd a jes bit my heart in two; foh it come bang in my mouf.

Reenter Joe.

Joe. Wal, nig, I've come back ter show yo the way t' a safe place. Come with me to yen village. [*Shouting in the distance.*] Whats all the row thar? Let's go. [*Exeunt.*

SCENE III. *A street in the village.   Citizens shouting and running.*

Enter JOE *and the negro.*

JOE.   What's up thar, boys?   What's in the wind?

    First CIT.   Have you not heard the news?   Fort Sumpter's fall'n.

Arm, brave boys, to arms!   Legion on legion
Let your strength pour in.   Our flag's insulted
By the haughty autocrat of slavery.
The lowering cloud that ominously
Hung o'er liberty's horizon at last
Has burst; and at the first concussion, while
The wires ache with burdens of this shameful
News, the drowsy North wakes from her slumbers
But to exchange her fitful dream of war
For grim reality; and now awaked
By cannon's boom, sees with eyes unhoodwink'd
The treach'rous nature of her enemies   .
Too long forborne; to see her dear old flag
Shot down, disgraced; her fair fame degraded
To be the scoff of jealous monarchies;
Derision of earth's kingdoms; since her great
Humanizing word "democracy" has
Prov'd a failure!   Oh, 'tis too much!   Th' insult's
Too deep; thousands, thousands, are springing at·
The hurt of mutual degradation to
To the shrine of war, calling for arms, leaders.
To arms!   To arms, Brave men!   With patriarch
Abraham, whose heart, like his grand purpose
Lies staunchly grounded as the bottom rock.
We'll hurl th' aggressive waves of slavery
Back against the foes who forge our gyves.

    Second CIT.   Come one and all, brave boys; dont let our village be behind the rest.   Rally round the flag.   You are safe with honest Abram Lincoln.

Joe. Boys, I'm up from old Kentuck, whar Abe Lincoln war born. [*Citizens gather round* Joe.] I hed a right smart uv a meetin' with 'im wunst, in Illinois an' he tole me some mighty sensible things. I know that ar man right wal; an' kin tell ye he's got the right pluck too. Ye kin bet high on that ar. I jes this minute made a cowardly sneak what attempted fur ter kidnap this yer nigger—I say I jes drummed 'im out o' camp to the tune of "Go you rogue you." Now, nig, whether yo air a runaway or no, yo ken fight fur yer freedom can't yer? Smash the rotten fugertive slave law! Will yer fight?

Quash. Yas, dat I'll do. Dat's a grand notion. Gorry, I'll smash some on em. I'se got many a scar on my back, but its stout enough yet to kerry a knapsack and gun.

Joe. Good on yer head, wooly, stay by me. I'll gin yer 'nuff fur to eat and drink jes fur that ar.

Third Cit. [*Aside*] Good loyal fellow, is that.

Joe. Come with me, my good feller, yo need refreshments. Yes, I knowed Abe Lincoln, an' I repeat, he's got the stuff in 'im.

[*Enter a messenger.*]

Mess. The president has issued a proclamation calling immediately for seventy five thousand men.

[*A marshall is seen taking enlistments. Fife and drum heard. Soldiers march through and return.*

Joe. Good! I told ye. That ar looks like war in dead airnest. I'll jes git up a company myself, though I'm getting to be an old man. I'll let the rebels see what an old backwoodsman kin do, a traitor huntin'. [*Exeunt* Joe *and the negro.*

First Cit. Let the enlistments go on as rapidly as possible. (*Curtain drops while music, marching and counter-marching is going on.*)

ACT III.

SCENE 1. *The fortifications and scenery on the battle-ground of Bull Run.*

Enter Civilians and COPPERHEAD.

COPPERHEAD.   WE are a jolly crowd from Wash-
    ington,
Arrived to view this battle on Bull Run,
And mark this onset of discordant war
'Twixt the green Yankee and ripe Southron power.
Ah!   In the distance hear the rattling sound,
As musket volleys through the woods resound.
Many a black Republican shall gasp,
Before this battle demon loose his grasp.
Oh, I do long to see my southern friends
Break from their thralldom—the vile, filthy dens
Of northern commerce, northern legislation,
Northern insult, taunt, slur, crimination,
E'en northern enterprise I'd fain see warr'd down,
While sacred slavery wafts a fair renown
From deep to deep; extending yet her sway
O'er the whole continent of America.
What can that crazy, apish Lincoln think?
Throwing his untrained rabble on the brink
Of fell destruction.   There he sits in state,
And from his usurp'd seat puffs fool's dictate
To mushroom generals, regardless of their plan
Suggested by the features of the land.
How can so great collision of men's brains
Fail to secure the vict'ry to our friends?

Oh, 'twas the crowning stroke of Yankee shave
To make a president of that worthless knave;
That tyrant; that folly babbling joker;
That rail-splitter and abolition croaker.
With no more mind to urge his flat brawl'd
    speeches,
Than the numb negro slave for whom he preaches.
Detestable, maudlin, ladder legged spy.
Oh had I adjectives to qualify
My abject loathing of that hated rat,
I'd torture language···· [*A bomb shell drops and
explodes.*] Wough, bah, run, boys, run!

First CIVILIAN. Gentlemen, that visitor comes
at a ruinous proximity. For my part I feel dis-
mayed. I can say I now see the point wherein
heels are more valuable than heads. [*Runs.*

Second CIV. It appears by the sound of the
battle that our forces are being driven by the enemy.

COP. I dont know whether to run or hide.
Zounds! It's a wonder that shell had'nt blown me
to "the undiscovered country from whose bourne no
traveller returns". I think I'll crawl in among the
rocks. Hark, ho! Run for life! The yankees are
whipped; retreating in confusion! [*Hiding*] Hello
there, every man of you; spread the alarm! The
rebels are upon us. [*Aside.*] But as I sympathize
with them I'll have nothing to fear.

    Enter JOE, *fighting his assailants. Confusion a-
mongst the civilians. Rebel war-cry heard advancing.*

    JOE. [*Struggling with superior numbers.*] Take
that ar, yo hairy cannibal. [*He dies.*] Courage men,
don't give way. Right about, face, charge! Come
on, yo black alligator. [*Strikes a rebel Captain rush-
ing on him.*] Ha, yo grazed me that ar time; hit'll
be the last time yer'll ever scratch ole Joe. Git

this an' chaw it till yer hide's as black as yer infarnal boss's down thar whar I send yo ter.

REBEL COLONEL.   Oh, I'm killed.   [*Dies.*]

JOE.   Yo mought uv expected as much.   I'll larn
yer.   Boys I'm a bleedin'.   The rebs is comin'.   Go
take care o' yerselves.   I'll be at yer head agin.
This yer scratch'll be uv small account.   [*Rebels
surround and take* JOE *and others prisoners.*]

Enter BEAUREGARD, DAVIS *and a courier on horseback.*

DAVIS.   Ah my brave, noble general; your wit
And wisdom win.

BEAU.   Here Courier, bear these dispatches quickly
To their several Heads.   Bid them proclaim to
Our brave troops my best congratulations
For this great vict'ry they have won for us.
[*Exit Messenger.*
Sir, let me thank you for this compliment
For I esteem it; coming as it does
From such a noble source.   Your hand is warm,
Glow'd from the furnace of a gushing heart.

DAV.   See how our heroes execute their oath
And scoop the craven cowards by thousands
Into the prisoners' list.   And those that do
Escape bear most lugubrious witness
In their bleeding flesh and broken bones
Of the reception they are to receive,
When brought to combat Southern Chivalry.
One more such victory will affright the
Northern mudsills to such a crestfall'n ebb
That they'll fret less their blind belligerence
And deem the thing most provident to yield
To their superiors.   Meanwhile remember
The sacred oath.   Keep dark the true design
Of this rebellion.   Let our brave warriors
Think they fight for life and absolution

From the hated North; for if they know 'tis
For a kingdom, 'twill breed disaffection.
Let th' imprison'd dogs be sent to Libby
And Castle Thunder; and there, entomb'd in
Noxious vaults, confederate with rats and
Batten on the offal of their worship'd
Nigger.   [Cop. *ventures cautiously from his conceal-*
ment and extends his hand to Davis.

Cop.   Greeting, old friends;
Glad to meet you here at this auspicious
Crisis.

Dav.   Who is he?   Was it not he came crawling
Like a flogg'd setter from amongst those rocks?
Stand, sir?   I think I've seen you somewhere!

Cop.   My dear sir, you feign forgetfulness.   Is
The past so blackly blackened that but this
Slender cord remains to bind our mem'ries?
I am much grieved at this oblivion.
There were times when in the yankee congress
We were both honored; on equal footing;
Spurred by like rank and princ'ple; each other's
Views reciprocated.   We hurled defiant
Language at abolition votaries
With whom our congress teemed.   'Twas a north-
ern
State I represented.   So much more credit
In ratio with the opposition met.

Beau.   Go over to the south and join the ranks.
We can't recognize you northern straddlers
Till you're purged of that stale infusion
Which makes you rancid to our moral tastes,
By formal action.

Dav.   I know you not.   My province it is not,
Placed in th' exalted quality I hold—
First magnate of a realm—to chatter
With the denizens of a defunct nation.

[*Turning to* B**eauregard**.]
Look to the int'rest of yourself and ours.
I'll in haste return to Richmond.   Farewell.
                        |*All except* Cop., *Exeunt.*
   Cop. Snubb'd again! I'm hated at north and south
And *I hate niggers.* But I'd better leave,
Lest there descend another omniburst
To freight me fee-taxed o'er Acheron's flood
That parts on Charon's rowcraft bad from good.
[*Another shell falls and explodes.*] Wough!   Terrors
and confusions!   Val, where art thou?   I see thee
not in the skies.   Such an eruption has scarcely been
known since the misfortune to Mr. Secundus Pliny.
The wildest theorist can shape no proof that I am
longer a breathing man.   Yet, I have faculties, body
and mind.   With my right hand I explore reason's
throbbing temple.   I feel of my legs with the left.
They are there.   I can stoop and touch the earth.
True, my confusion forbids the collected judgment
I'm wont to use; I have been a man of standing. I
am now a man standing.   I see, feel and hear.   Ergo, I am unblown.   Horrific as was the explosion,
spasmodic as was the effect, I will attempt to run.
Yet when I bethink me of that concussion I reason
afresh.   Firstly: a bomb shell bursts close to my
very heels!   It were madness to suppose its frag-
ments had not mopped mine to the whirlwinds!   A
thing like it was never known.   I judge from precedent.   Ergo, I am blown, and am not here.   Perhaps a head, an arm, a leg, parts of a mutilated
trunk are scattered about the battleground as evi-
dence that I was killed in battle.   Honorable of
course.   But one argument remains in my favor;
I have long had a presentiment that on the event
of my taking off, I should immediately feel pain
and stifling suffocation as of fire; be made sensible

to this; that long-fingered, grim visages would disgust me with their skinny obtrusions. But I see, now, feel no pain; ergo, I live—either through an unexpectedly propitious dispensation of Providence if dead, or else by the miraculous fact that I am corporeally alive! I decide in favor of the latter— I live, therefore I run. One, two, three and away.

[Exit.

SCENE II. *A parlor in the White House.* MARY *and* ADELINA, *wives to* LINCOLN *and* SEWARD.

ADEL. Why?

MARY. Oh, the perplexities of his situation much more than counterbalance the value of mere honors.

ADEL. Do you not think, my dear friend, that he is happier, as chief magistrate, with the eye of the world upon him than ever before?

MARY. Far from it. Often have I heard him mention that his happiest days were those when we were tranquilly partaking the blessings of our humble home. He thinks there are no sweeter pleasures than those obtained from domestic life.

ADEL. But do you not think it was ambition that led him from this life of quietude to the position he now holds? You are aware that people become ambitious when they lose contentment. Ambition may be pronounced the parent of discontent. There must have been a spark of ambition gnawing deep in his heart that kindled into a flame as opportunity offered it fuel.

MARY. I understand you, my dear, perfectly; but I think I can say Mr. Lincoln was not prompted by ambition; that is, not by selfish motive. It was duty. He always seemed to be laboring under an impression that he had a great duty to perform; and therefore, I doubt not, he would have been unhappy had he not fulfilled that requirement.

Enter LINCOLN, *the President and* SEWARD, *his Secretary.*

SEW. A pleasant evening, ladies, which you are doubtless enjoying. Perhaps our intrusion interrupts an enlivening colloquy.

LIN. Ladies have their peculiarities; but is it a peculiarity in them to be annoyed by any intrusion their husbands can make?

ADEL. No, no, sir. Indeed, you are perfectly right.

LIN. You see the point I am aiming at?

SEW. I apprehend your drift but your points are well veiled from my vision.

LIN. Intrusions are interruptions, but this don't make interruptions intrusions. Here you have both a point and a blunt. Do you now see?

SEW. I confess to the main statement but do not grasp the logical application.

LIN. Well, intrusions are supposed to be sharp, of course. and solid; else they would not intrude.

SEW. Yes yes, there is a point. Well, "go in".

LIN. The interruption is a synonym of bluntness as its name implies;—broken off. Now sir, as your worshiped Arabians have absorbed the undue gossip of a large public, including amateurs, naturalists and ladies who arrogate to themselves the right to compare such beauty with that of a statesman's nose or the president's face, thus questioning our championship for ugliness, it is time those rivals were fenced from the world's gaze. Just give me a commander and line and out of the two principles, the sharp and blunt, I will build them a stake-an'-ridered pen.

SEW. Ladies, a joke in the wind, at the expense of my celebrated, imported ponies! Please sir, build my fence immediately.

LIN. Easily done. I have made many a fence

out of tougher stuff. Now, mark; the ground whereon I build is the logic; the interruptions the rail-cuts, split into fence-rails. I am the railsplitter.

MARY. But, Mr. Lincoln......

LIN. Please don't interrupt me, ma'am, now that I am farming again. Upon a logical basis I would erect my fence even unto the seventh rail in hight.

ADEL. But without interrupting, I must confess that your points though they may be logical enough, to me are exceedingly dull. Aren't you a bore?

LIN. Intrusions are sharp; though no joke, yet they drive; hence my fence-stakes. A little muscle and with my commander in hand the stakes are driven "deep in the mellow ground" and the rider put on its crossings. Thus you have a fence, strong and high enough to hold your arabians safe.

SEW. I see, yet cannot see.

LIN. Then you must be multiplying more in years than vision.

SEW. Pardon, I see your kindness yet cannot see why our entrance here is not an interruption and an intrusion upon the ladies' courtesy.

LIN. Well, I may venture to explain that in a few words. Rougher material might have been intrusive; but you observe our abrupt presence becomes not only unintrusive but really desirable.

MARY. Let me repeat, to stay further warping of fancies, that we do most welcome your coming.

ADEL. And further; that this interrupting be
Forever broken, thus gaining two points
Where before was one, let's call to mind the
The subject of our chatting before your
Gallant entry.

LIN. Eigh, ho, this is the prettiest hit of all!
I could materialize, magician-like,
Weave wood-webs with wordy woof and filling,

To box a statesman's ponies up with rails
Of sophistry and pasture them in clover
Scented syllogism, yet fail to have the
Captious slight of changing subjects.   Ladies,
Please resume.

ADEL.   We were quizzing life's droll vicissi-
    tudes—
Whether it were ambition, fate or chance
That coaxed you from an unpretending home
Of comforts, free from the calumnies which
Embitter fame and made you chief of chiefs.

MARY.   I argued it was duty, not fortune.
Fortune it is not to buffet hardships
Which do cincture offices like yours.

ADEL.   And I, that 'twere ambition.   Is it not
The steppingstone to greatness?   What though fate's
Rough acclivities, beset with toils, shall
Hoist a scowling front!   Does it not well
Repay in doing right, sweet consciousness
Possessing that angels smile?   For though of
Gaze the cynosure from mortal millions,
Still, in well-doing you live down the whims
And criticisms of the bad, gaining
Pleasure from the good.   Accept a woman's
Judgment, that honest ambition is the
Prompter to all good works.

LIN.   Ha, here is woman's logic?   Well, proceed.

MARY.   I argued 'twere premonitory sight,
Or inspiration; or a conception
Germed in early youth, which with its stilly
Voice was ever breathing duty.   Service
Must be rendered unto humanity.

LIN.   Whether true or untrue your views may be,
They're prettily expressed and pictured;
Yet all my actions are most badly managed.
I feel I've 'scaped your scowling brain-rack—

The qualms of legislation— when I repair
To the sweet temple of domestic life,
Free from the realm of censure. Don't you think
Now, that a jolly joke, ruddy and rolling,
Round with ripeness, his very eye choking
With strains to be demure, is, when your brain is
Furloughed, the most refreshing physic for
Soul and body?

    ADEL.   Oh you invet'rate joker! What a point!
A pity 'tis you weren't wedded to
A joke.

    SEW. Pshaw, he can consolidate them into women.

    MARY. You really amaze me!

    SEW.   Nay, but 'tis true.
He chrystalizes imagery, forsooth.
He'd use legerdemain or dialectic
Jugglery to transform ether into
Solid shapes.

    MARY. Now I, myself, am fond of jokes and tales.

    LIN. My dear, thou rallyest when perchance
I'm cornered. I'm of opinion
Thou wert created of a joke. Ribs are
Too crook'd and brittle for thy unswerving
Nature which bends not nor breaks ; but like the
Heroic pun, when I'm attacked by stronger
Powers, or nettled, thou parryest for my
Rescue. Therefore, thou'rt of the refreshing
Joke most typical—a doctor, lawyer,
Teacher.

    SEW. How prove you that jokes possess pro-
            fessions ?
Lawyers I always knew were jokes, but didn't
Know that jokes were lawyers.

    ADEL. My dear. you are confessing much, to say
You are an object to cause merriment.

    LIN. Ah, madam, know you that he still is and

has been, a target at which the saucy
Waggery of millions aims.　Scarce a round
Year since he proclaimed his prophecy of
Conflicts irrepressible.　The bluff world
Has racked sarcasm and laughter; not at the
Word, which is fast reaching consummation,
But at the poor man, its author.　He must
Be forced to run the gauntlet, while puffing
Punsters, poets, pipers, pedants, punch, pound
And poke, proceeding with firebrand-satirists'
Couplets; and bruise, spear, harass him throughout
The grim ordeal; he, writhing with the
Scorch, they fiercely happy at their baseless
Wit.　But I am glad you have your share; you
Better can esteem my misery.　If
They poke fun at you, I shan't object; for
I do love the people and will not blame
Them, though they have amidst them a thousand
Juvenals

ADEL.　Now, sir unraveler, give us your wisdom;
That we may know how playful tongue-warp'd wind
Disguises its aerial nature and
Is transformed to doctors, lawyers, teachers.

LIN.　Mark.　Take first a case of indigestion;
A misery harborer; its subject lean,
Wan and woebegone;—a bleach'd recipient
Of nightmare.　A statue-ruin-Bacchus.
Suppose I were his doctor, what would I do?

ADEL.　I think you'd drain his system with a
　　　course
Of physic.　You are systematic,　What
　　　would he do?

MARY.　I think your patient would be petted and
Dosed with anodynes and cordials and given
Strict injunctions not to leave his room, which
By your tender care would be replete with

Roses and other scented flowers, in such
Profusion as to form an aromatic
Halo round his head.
    LIN. No such thing I'd do; but I would make
      him
Sore with laughter; taxing my genius
To produce fresh jokes and drollery; and
Operate upon his risibles with
Puns and jolly tales; deny him every
Aliment except his crust and gruel;
And though my shriveling hovered o'er the grave,
Health would soon buoy him like th' enfranchis'd
      slave.
    SEW. I now believe in the metempsychosis!
Give us your hand, Asclepias. Ladies,
A reëmbodiment of Hypocrates!
Sound in hygienic lore.
    MARY. My dear, with all your droll facetiousness
And runnic levity, I see your heart
Is troubled.
    LIN. Sweet friends, can I be alone? Another
      time
I will resume my lecture and discuss
The consanguinity of jokes and pedagogues.
    SEW. [*To ladies.*] He's been sad all day with
      some foreboding.
Let us retire and leave him to his thoughts.
               [SEW., ADEL. *and* MARY, *exeunt.*
    LIN. If to disguise is wrongful, then am I
Dishonest. Oh, I am tortured with the
Gashes of my countrymen! They, on the
Humid field, like heroes contending for
Th' insulted flag. Ah, and this moment in
The lunge of battle! Whilst purple streams do
Clot and clog the channels of Bull Run; I,
Midst luxuries palatial, like the turk,

Enjoying what my conscience denies me,
Partaking what my nature would reject.
Such is my heart's reciprocation, that
I seem to feel the slashing sabers and
Th' impetuous bullet, the pond'rous
Shot and detonating shell, crashing and
Plowing through flesh, bone and brain! But ah, as
Rallying contemplation taunts me, I lounge
Idling; placed here to head them, too weak to
Fend and powerless to bear their mortal pains,
Studying some driv'ling joke, unsacred,
Tame, irrelevant to this whirlpool of
Issues, to blockade maudlin tears, 'tis then
I feel responsibility and great
Unworthiness.   [*Shouts of citizens. Commotion
        on the grounds in view through the corridors.*
    First CIT.   The battle!   The battle!
    Second CIT.   What of the battle? All goes well.
        The last
Dispatches proclaimed us on the brow of
Victory.
    LIN.   Dispatches are double-tongued.   They flat-
        ter.
Ah, my forebodings have not been misshaped!
    Third CIT.   The town's caught rumors of a hol-
        ocaust!
A wholesale sacrifice!   Ten thousand men!
Disaster!   Our whole army's butchered, souls
Unnumbered.   The Black-horse-cavalry, an
Og'rish tribe of creole giants, with but
One tooth in each jaw, which, like the snapping-
Turtle's finishes the set, and beards from
Weird visages depending half a yard.
Fresh hurried from the howling wolf-dens of
The Mississippi, in drag'nish trappings,
Came clattering, bellowing down upon

Our inexperienced regiments, dealing
Them deadly thrusts. Our bloodshot warriors
Wavered and shrank back. Ere their captains could
Effect a rally, a thousand cowardly
Civilians whom curiosity had drawn
From Washington and all the points about,
Struck up, as by preconcert, confusion's
Scare; making such fiendish yells and scrambling,
That quailing, our terrified combattants
Broke rank and in a mob were cut and sluiced
Like squabs. The conquerers have snared them in
For game!
    MESSENGER. The Buck-tails! The Buck-tails, our
        choicest hope!
The Buck-tail regiment a thousand strong,
Enlisted from the Alleghenies; a
Pick of seven foot giants, inured to work,
Got tangled in a deep decoy, sly set 'mongst
Cloughs and pocket-gulfs of old Bull Run and
Lassoed, bowie-knifed, bludgeoned by the Black
Horse cavalry! To arms! It is the worst,
Cruelest dead-fall since Hasdrubal's *chute.*
        [*Citizens exeunt passing along the grounds.*
    LIN. I saw it, felt it years ago; dreaded,
Hoped that heaven would stay the deadly blow
That Satan raised.

        Re-enter SEWARD. *with ladies.*

    SEW. Tidings are most sad, good friend, but you are
Overtaxed. Go take some rest. You need it;
And I....
    LIN. No. I must hence. My Country bleeds. It is
My purpose to multiply our legions;
For I'm convinced that to repel the force
Arrayed against us, will consume many
Armies. I'll summon them. No traitor shall
Trample the flag my people honor. Adieu. [*Exit.*

SCENE IV. *Idem. A Rumhole.*

Enter several rummies.

BOB. Heigh, ho, this whisky tastes sharp of the tart that makes and takes!

BILL. What?

BOB. Here, Bill, take another jumper an' I'll tell ye. No, I'd better let ye guess.

BILL Well, it makes one feel good, as ye see. Wasn't that a scientific shuffle? Here's what it makes. [*Sings and dances.*

Merry ho, ho,
Tripping the toe,
Fal de rol, tal de rol, heigh, ho,
Many's the day
That I've tippled away
With merry ho, heel and toe, gay.

BOB. Hic, Yer git'n boozy, Bill; so am I an' I confess it's a shame.

BILL. If I guess right, I'm sober; if wrong, I'm hic, intox....

BOB. Well,

BILL. Well, it makes merry; and it takes the "do-dads"; but afore this nigger war's over, it'll take yer pocket full jes to git yer whistle wet.

BOB. Yes, but no.

BILL. Explain yerself.

BOB. Yes, it'll make merry an' cost money. It's a fact; but that isn't all whisky can do. It can make drunkards an' take their lives. A hog's too
[*Enter* COP., *puffing, exhausted and drabbled.*
sens'ble to swill it an' Bill, I'm goin' to take a lesson in health from a hog an' swill whisky no more.

BILL. Robert, hic, We have been friends. We are now enemies. Ye coolly insinnivate that I'm worse 'n a swine bein' as ye know I'm drunk. I don't thank nuther you nur whisky fur breakin'

up our 'quaintance, but I'm goin' to 'spostilate agin'
bein' called a hog or a black abolitionist. I propose
to smash yer, hic, snoot, Robert, or somebody's else
jes te lay this volcano of fire-water an' wrath!

Bob. The president has issued a proclamation,
calling for three hundred thousand more Union volunteers. I'm one o' them and this is my last spree.

Bill. Bob, you're crazy! If you're in such a
hurry to die why don't you go and hang yerself and
die decent? D'ye want to blacken yer conscience
first, by jinin' that abolitionist rabble? Can't ye take
warnin' o' this Bull Run ruin?

Cop. Here, landlord, give me a glass best bran-
dy. Say, youngsters, what did I hear you prating?

Bill. That's fine comment for a drounded rat. I
say, ole plug, where did ye git that coat o' paint?
Ye're as yaller as a California mountain an' I spose
ye know that's black. Wash the outside an' 't'll
turn yaller an' so will you. But I'd hate to be the
one to scrub you down to the real skin color. He'll
find his gold washin' is more precious in color than
value....

Cop. By the fierce grimalkins!

Bill. Say fifteen hundred.

Cop. Wretch, I will stab thee for thy insolence!
                    [Bob *rushes between them.*]

Bill. The price of a buck negro.

Cop. Off, let me strike the polecat!

Bob. No, he's mad with drinks.

Cop.   Shades of the mighty!
Have I groped all the distance from Bull Run,
Half way with murd'ring rebels at my heels,
And braved the perils of the first campaign,
Been blown to shivers by the slicing shells
Which dropped like Ætna's cinders on men's toes,
Been fire-besmirched of powder, snubbed by friends

And made to save the remnant left me of
Life, scatter'd senses, limbs and rags, by
Dint of a retreat as slop-grimed as 'twas speedy,
To be insulted by such scratch-heads?

BILL.   Shall I kill him?   See; he's one o' yer
brave abolitionists, toadying for Abraham, the patriarch.   Here, soap-grease, I guess I'll cut your
weazand for ye—let out some o' that hurricane.   I
see ye're a'swellin' up an' bilin' over like a scorch-
ed bubble.

BOB.   William, we have been friends.   Don't let
us become enemies.   I know your condition and
forgive you; but don't let me hear any more railing
on the president.

[COP. *stands jesticulating.*

COP.   Gods!   I was jaded but a moment since.
'Tis too much!   My brain!   This indignation
Burns me; caused by that foul aspersion.   Fiend!
Did you name me abolitionist?   Oeough!
Thing, wert thou but my equal I would mop
This gin-mill with thee till thou hadst not brawn
To bawl for succor.

BILL.   Hello!   That sounds demercrat.   Ef you
be, hic, guess I'll not strangle ye.   Gi' me yer paw.

COP.   So?   Have I fall'n among friends?   Are all
here, democrats?

LANDLORD.   Yes, good friend, to be sure.   Boys,
use him well.   A gentleman, ha!

BILL.   Ho, you're smutty for a demercrat; but I
see; it's the effect of bein' among them 'malgama-
tionists.   Here, hic, come, my treat, all 'round to
the company.   Landlord, give this gentleman a stout
one.   He thinks more of the white man than he
does of the nigger.   Here's luck to the southern
chivalry!   Hurrrah for the southern chivalry!
Hurrah, hurrah!   [*All shout and drink, except* BOB.

Bob.   I'm sick and 'shamed that I've so long argued and drank for the democracy. A principle
run mad!

Cop. .Were't not that I belong to higher rank,
    I'd.....

Bob.   Don't brag of high rank.   Men are all on
a low level in the grog-hole.

Cop.   What, a spy! [*To* Bill.]   Is it safe here ?

Bill.   Pshaw!   He's an old friend.   Whiskey
makes him cross.   Don't notice him.

Cop. [*Aside.*] I'll take new courage, then. [*Aloud.*
    Friends, I have a
Magazine within me, of seething hate.
B, bu, but patience!   When I think of my
Great injuries, I'm choked.   I am, in halls
Of Congress, esteemed most eloquent.   Now,
Mad reflection chokes me.   I can but rail
And imprecate.   The leering demagogue
And his. pilf"ring bloodsuckers!   He's wheedled
Himself to the chief magistracy when
Conscious of the consequences ; and now
Sits spitting blood contemptuously into
The very face of scores of millions. too
Flush'd with selfish policy to smell the
Blood he spills.   Lincoln's a murderer !

Bill.   Why don't you call 'im suthin'? Now jest
hear me name 'im.   Take an injin, a nigger. a baboon, a carrion buzzard, a fool, mad dog, rattlesnake,
catamount, skunk and a hyena.   Chuck 'em all into one cage.   Let 'em eat one another up till there's
nothin' left.   The quintessence of that pizen nothin', biled down fur dog's-bane, is old Abe Lincoln.

Omnes.   Ha ha ha !   [*Exit* Bob.

Cop.   You have relieved me.   Thank you,
My treat this time.   You're ahead.   Come.

                Enter Florence, *lost sister to* Joe.

FLOR. Gentlemen, I am directed hither with assurance that you are friends of the Confederacy.

COP. Ha, faith! You are right mam'selle. We esteem the Confederacy as we esteem the fair; and we esteem beauty above virtue. Who are you? Some bonny lass upon whom gentlemen execute charity? Pardon an ambiguity, miss.

FLOR. Sir, your insinuation is too scurrilous to proceed from the lips of a gentleman.

COP. Egad! Another bluff, or I'm salt and pepper. Madame, most respectfully. What would you have us do?

FLOR. I wish letters of introduction to General Beauregard.

COP. Ha, Beauregard! Position has enlarged Him. Two short months ago we were acquaint'.
I, his adviser. His conversation
Then, so liquid that it rolled on fussy
Axles, oiled with obsequious smiles. But ah!
I saw him yesterday with Davis, at
The battle. Success them so inflated
That they knew me not. I relish not this
Arrogance; and question propriety
In giving aid and comfort to vapid
Braggarts. But lady, state your object and
Be sure I'll work you service

FLOR. One side, kind sir. The first accost was, as
I thought, ungenerous. Let my abrupt
Obtrusion at your revels cancel ill humors.

COP. Thank you, thank you, sweet woman,
your kindness
Overflows.

FLOR. I much sympathize with those determin'd
Heroes; and since the outbreak, being young
And full of health and love of wild adventure,
Have bethought me 'twere no disgraceful task
To lend my friends assistance, as a spy.

Cop. Ut, tut, tut, lady! I'm confounded at
Your daring. You, so young and pretty, a
Spy? The Yanks will hang you on a gibbet.
Flor. I take the consequence. Will you aid me?
Cop. Lady, you put a pungent question. This
Plight you see me in, deceives my state.
I'm of the yankee Congress. I have power
To lend you furtherance and will. Exchange
Addresses with me. We'll be friends. [*She exchan-
    ges cards with him. Noise outside, approaching.*
Hark? [*Aside.*] Conscience surrenders me. My
    legs shall
Not. Oeough! The soul rebels against the body.
                                [*Hides behind counter.*

Re-enter Bob., *with officers.*

Bob. Here, Captain, seize the mutinous rabble.
                                [*Soldiers arrest them.*
Land. Say, villian, your excuse for this.
Bob. I am no villian, sir. I am a soldier. My
business is to bag the enemy; but my excuse for
being here is that you are northern rebels. You
reviled the President in the teeth of my caution-
ing—called him a murderer. You are full of treason and dangerous, cowardly auxiliaries to the Confederacy. The President has ordered the suspen-
sion of the writ of habeas corpus; and directs that
all such traitors be immediately arrested and sent to
Fort Lafayette and other prisons where they can do
no harm. Where's that bragging old traitor?
Officer. Out with them, men. Look here miss,
you had better go away. This is rough business
for you to witness. [*Exeunt omnes
            except* Cop., *who cautiously emerges.*
Cop. By all the Fates! Escaped again. Can it
Be possible I was created to
Survive this threat'ning brigandage? Why, my

Life is charmed! Hush! I'm yet vulnerable; but
My cause is right. Nay, Val, be honest to thyself.
Thou knowest that thou liest. Thou'rt on the
Fence, divaricate; yet one foot dangleth
Lowest toward the South. First, skulked behind a
Rock and next a counter! It must be said
Thou'rt fortunate; yet 'tis amazing that
Thou escap'st detection. Surely, it was
Beyond their comprehension that thou couldst
So belittle thy estate, as to court
Refuge in such snakish attitudes! Then
Thy magnanimity hath saved thee! Not
Thine, but that th'ingenuous world accrediteth
Thee. Val, thou'rt a knave; a snake with beaut'ous
Tints and noiseless locomotion and gemmy
Eyes of fascinating power; sly, gifted,
Artful, yet indifferent; and fang-jawed;
Whose hollows secrete a deadly venom.
Thou'rt not a rattlesnake; for he doth give
Some omen of his presence; as 'twere a
Whizzing quiver of remorse, which strains
The tendons of a fiend's resolve to such
Fell tension that his very organism
With rigidity excessive, trembles;
Clanks aloud the monster's scales, that innocence
May take warning. But thou'rt a copperhead;
Prone crawling o'er the grass; subtile and still;
Refusing to betray, e'en by malignant
Hiss, his nearness, till the doom'd victim feels
The poison'd tooth and dies. A copperhead;
And all of thy coadjutors; hated
Of the friends thou wouldst assist.
Sting, then; bite and hide thy creeping nature;
For if thou lettest the nation know thy heart
Thou'llt die an outlaw. Woe betide the craven
Who pronounces sentence which consigns to

Banishment and dungeons, the innocents
Who dare speak their thoughts! A reign of terror!
       [*Noise without and* Cop. *alarmed, exit.*

    Scene V. *Richmond. A cell in Libby Pris-*
on. Prisoners in tatters and woe. Florence *re-*
garding Joe *in chains.*

    Flor. Ah, I see him, but he knows me not. 'Tis
The same rough man of deeds, whose valor charms
Me. A mate was never mated. A man
By fiends unmanned. See how he stoops to breast
His heavy thongs! Excused shall be the maiden's
Heart that's won by manhood's nature-vested
Title. Though a rough exterior, with
Age and bony frame and language uncouth,
With wrinkl'd brow and silver-setting locks,
Yet many's the soul longs for her Jason
Who bravely gives his life for liberty.
Traitors to my country, ye call me spy!
Well, I will ply a maiden's wiles and use
The juggler's art and scare these murd'rers, by
Warping their craven superstitions with
Apparitions weird. My work shall be, while
On this espionage, to dress the wounds
And calm the agony of suffering
Victims of the fell fiend of war.'

    Enter Davis, Winder *and* Turner.

    Davis. Sir, let us dispatch our reconnoissance.
'Tis a fetid dungeon. The air is mixed
With noxious putrefactions; and the eye
Meets objects that appall. Bah! One's stomach
Nauseates. The brain gets dizzy at the
Contemplating. You have well executed
My commands, good General. The dusty
Floor well animates with vermin; the putrid
Emanations and the wan spectres that
Haze about the vaults—a foul congeries

Of blight!   'Tis good offspring of your genius.
Well done.   Here is a purse of gold.   I'll hence.
　　Wind.   Thank you, lord President; but you've
　　　　missed the
Half of their excruciate glum.   Allow me
Most rev'rently, to individualize:
Here is a man—get up, you bleach'd,
Attenuated tail of Satan; else
By the gods. we'll cudgel every ray of
Life and light from those old skin-bone ruins!—
This is a man, gulched in the last quivers of
Starvation.
　　Davis.   [*Aside.*]   The oath I took to serve the
　　　　devil, was
An atrocity!   Friends, let's quit this antrum
Of effluvia.
　　Wind.   Nay. noble potentate, tarry awhile;
And you shall further gloat on sights to charm
The demons.   View yonder group.   They have been
Sullen, refractory and wilful.   On
Them have I devoted special malice.
Here. Captain, whip them up; let Wirtz assist;
And if they feign debility, or lag.
Or cringe, or twist the ponderous gyves which
Shackle them, why, flay them till they beg.
　　Dav.   [*Pointing to* Joe.]   General, how's this?
Those northern brags so drained of stock they must
Needs send to fight our chivalry, such a
Cadaverous hoosier?   An aged rainbow
With the colors faded!　　　[*Hunting* Joe., *bent
　　　　and emaciated, is dogged forward.*
　　Omnes.   Ha, ha. ha, ha.
　　Dav. Sure, there be signs of rain.   A nimbus true,
Whose presence doth betoken dampness; as
These humid, malaria-infected gusts
Do testify.   Ha, ha; I'm sure 'twill rain;

For water thickens on my lids from damps
And laughter! Ha, ha, ha, ha, a trembling
Septuagenarian. Bah! Sent here to
Measure strength with men! The idea!

TURN. The idea! Truly, 'tis laughable;
But ideas are not oak. Yon gaunt clown well
Can illustrate it. He's the most dreaded
Subject in the cells. [*Wirtz and his posse urge the
prisoners forward.* FLORENCE *advances to* DAVIS.

FLOR. The genius of charity weeps for the
Innocent. Canst thou regard their tortures with-
    out shame?
The gates of hell seem shoved aside that thou
May'st gaze and hug this nucleous of sin.
And thou sav'st them not? Nay, even addest;
Gloating on this massive wrong, thou cumb'rest
Worse thy guilt. Have mercy, then, oh, creature
Graced with power and rescue those perishing
Men.

DAV. What, who, whence is this? A spirit or a
Dream?

WIRTZ. Faster, ye dronish crawfish, or I'll brain
ye! Here, turnkey, thump that hog-eyed sluggard
up. He's got a wicked look.

JOE. Look'ee, ye devil-fish 'o the traitors! Hit
me, an' ye will! Hit'll be the last time ye'll ever
hit. [*Turnkey strikes him.*] Thar, take that. [*Strikes
him down with his manacles.*] That ar's the way
I doom traitors. Off, I say, bewar'! [*To* FLORENCE.
Say, gal, ye're right smart uv roughin' it. Wal, yo'd
better git away, ef yo air made uv meat an' blood,
fur hit's no use pleadin' ter them treacherous brutes.
[*To others.*] Back! Tetch me not. Wot I say, I'll
stick to.

TURN. Ho, men, seize him! Take him out and
hang him, hang him, hang him to the nearest tree!

JOE.   Stan' back I say thar. I'll soon sarve ye
the same as that wuthless traitor lyin' thar. Whar's
the coward rebel as'll dare meet a union man on e-
qual terms? Ye haint a sprinklin' o' human blood
in ye. Ye yellin' cannibals. Ye sponge-headed cut-
throats! An' if I call ye alligators, I dont git down
half way to whar ye are; o'ny the scales what kiv-
ers ye keeps out the pricks o' conscience an' makes
ye wusser an' crueler'n a brute injin, an' yer sneakin' natur's indicative o' the crawlinest part uv an'
alligator's belly. Ye're hissin' snakes, allus doin' the
devil's will. Back I say! I would'nt fight ye on
terms any more'n I'd fight a woman ; but if ye tetch
me, ye're wilted corpses instanter.

WIND.   Seize that man, I say and have his neck
stretched.

JOE.   Back! thar, and thar, and thar.
                        [*A guard falls each blow.*
WIND.   What ho! Guards!

Enter more guards and officers.

Sieze that man and have him hanged on the instant.
   [*Confusion in which* JOE *is at last overpowered.*
Exeunt omnes except DAVIS, FLORENCE *and prisoners.*

DAVIS.   Most fearful episode! My opinions
Have undergone a metamorphosis.
He is a frightful character and I
Confess, fearless as I claim to be, I
Feel the ague jar of terror. Ho Guards!

Re-enter guards.

Take up those fallen jailors and straightway
Proceed to have that fellow hanged.
                        [*Exeunt guards with the dead men.*
FLOR.   [*Approaching.*] Sir, 'tis with tears and
        agony of heart,
That I approach thee on behalf of these
Poor prisoners. I only ask that thou

Wouldst amend that dread decree of torture
As to grant one little crust; some cooling
Beverage; and if thou wouldst not spare the
Pains to have their cell cleansed of this sickly
Mire, pray condescend to give them water;
That gladly they may minister to their
Own comforts. Death were a welcome chapter
To seal up the book of their existence.
But oh, to dwindle in slow starvation!
Life, at best, an oblique moonbeam, gleaming
Obscurely through fate's weeping clouds; but
Oh, to scatter poisons which infect its
Haze to greenness; to vitiate their clammy
Vault-air with blighting miasmata! tis
Too much for reflection. What then to be
Endured! Oh!....

DAVIS. Away, thou mystic sprite! Thou'rt no
    mortal
Thou art my conscience. I will repel thee. Go!

FLOR. Nay, do not repress her gentle tapping.
Let not thy heart lie cased within its bars.
Oh, for its own sake, let it yield unto
Compassion's promptings; for of thy short-liv'd
Gloatings which do yield a sickly
Satisfaction, there cometh a bitter end.

DAVIS.   Genius,
Avaunt! Wouldst thou allure a magnate of .
My potency by wheedling sophistry?
Folly, folly, folly. Screech not to me   [*She vanishes.*
Again. [*Aside,*] I'm damned!
        [*Noise of fire-arms and shouts without.*

Re-enter WINDER *and* TURNER.

WIND. Your Excellency, he has escaped.
DAVIS. How's that? Who?
WIND. The prisoner, Joe, the Hunter.
DAVIS. I'll give a glittering thousand for his

Body, dead or alive.   How did he 'scape?

TURN.   He wrenched the iron manacles from his
Wrists with a prodigious strength as only
Giants and madmen wield.....

DAVIS   What!   Are his fetters broken?   He's
   at large?

TURN.   And dashing the brains from some half
   dozen
Soldiers, scaled all barring obstacles, and
Fled uninjured through a storm of balls.

DAVIS.   Bestir the City guards.   Blockade all outs.
Spare no time or force, in his recapture.
Take the most dang'rous of these prisoners
And let them, in Low Moor shackles, welded
At Vulcan's forge, be, under escort of
This Wirtz, our modern Torquemada and
Prince of cruelties, man-wolf and pocket-
Heart, dragged South to denizen the Black-Holes
Of sunburnt Andersonville.   [*To prisoners.*]   Lie
   there, ye
Rotting miscreants of the North; and mold and
Bleach and wilt.   I'll rest secure in knowing
Ye're unmanned.

[FLORENCE *re-appears, at whom* DAVIS *stares,
while slowly following* WINDER *and* TURNER *out.
As* FLORENCE *slowly vanishes, the prisoners set up
a melancholy cry, while mournful music grows louder and louder.*]   [*Curtain falls.*

ACT IV.

SCENE I. *Washington. A public walk.*

Enter several rebel sympathizers in conversation.

BILL. Yes, and the draft.

HARMON. It will glean every man; rake the land clean from ocean to ocean.

BILL. As true as I hold position, that old hypocrite shall never get me into his clutch, so long as there's a Canada.

HARM. Do you imagine what is the sentiment of the community, just now? Why, I overheard a man saying that sooner than lose his liberty by being kidnapped, or drafted, like a convict, into the war, to kill, or be killed, by his friends, he would enter a conspiracy of assassination. Here he is.

THUG. Caution, caution! Do you imagine, sir, that to stanch the source-fountains of trouble, at once, would be a blessing?

HARM. Confidentially, I think so. Why, man? Do me the favor to bare your heart.

THUG. I've an omen he'll not disturb you long.
There's a muggy gust afloat. A murky
Breeze sniffs up from hell, wafting a crooked
Meaning; which 'tis not a public function
To divine.

Enter COP.

COP. Well, good morning, friends.
Ah, here's our unravel'd mystery of
Histrionic art—can play two games at
Once. How fare you? What's the news?

THUG. Domestically fair, socially passable,
Politically, disastrous.
He, he, he; glorious, rather.

Cop. And my sympathizing friend, how are you?

Bill. Oh, I am racked with pains. My eyes are bleared, my legs are cramped with rheumatism. I have an affection of the spine. In short, I am an offering of disease, within and without. What may be the hearsay about the draft?

Thug. [*Aside.*] There's a coward!

Cop. Bad, bad, dismal. The bloodthirsty Congress passed it, Lincoln has signed it, it Becomes a law.

Harm. Yes, and he'll need a dozen drafts to aid Him. The conqu'ring armies of General Lee Are pouring invasion into our State. Lee has recrossed the river.

Thug. Lee crossed the Potomac?

Cop. Aye, and herein lies disaster. Lee is As bold as skillful. He is a second Hannibal; and what he undertakes, that Will he execute.

Bill. I, I, I'm a little fearful We've no Mc-Clellan to defend us any more. Oh, the North is ruined! Well, the sooner the quicker. Let them come.

Cop. Yes, our McClellan's martyred. All is Disaster. Bad luck seems incorporate in, And forms a constituent of the old Dictator's make-up. Each plan he tries brings Swift discomfiture. From Sumpter to the Draft laws. Hideous retrospect! Two crazy Somersaults at Bull Run, which their dripping Reekings blend with crimson, gushing from the Gashes of consanguine neighbors—the twins Of Fredericksburg. And the red stream rolls on, Broadened by previous conflux with Ball Mound, Seven days, Antietam, until the tepid Flood assumes proportions huge and horrid

As the swath of cholera; and now, by
Fresh invasion, bears ogling netherward
A nation damned!

Enter LINCOLN.

THUG. Ah, what a dismal dream!

LIN. Friends, are you dreaming?

COP. I wish it were a dream.

LIN. Dreams are follies of imagination.
A greeting. I remember you. [THUG, *sneering,
shakes his head. The two sympthizers are won.*

COP. [*Pompously.*] Friends, respectfully; this
is the President.

THUG. [*Aside.*] Royal opportunity! I might
strike and
Consummate this business, now. I'll do it.
No, the plot; 'twont do; must wait. [*Exit* THUG.

COP. Your frankness makes me bold to say our
thoughts
Do not course in one channel.

LIN. I would that men might always think alike.
Your bloody river would dry up.

COP. But as 'tis, will you have it ever flow?

LIN. I would arrest its progress had I power.

COP. But all things augur ill. What purpose
you?

LIN. We propose to stand upon our dignity like
the boy down in Kentucky, who stubbed his toe
so severely that he stopped and stood trembling,
when another boy asked him why he did'nt cry.
he answered "I'm too big to cry and my toe aches
so bad I can't laugh". We mean to grin and stick.

COP. If I am impudent I beg pardon.
But tell me if there's aught but mischief in
That proclamation.

LIN. The slave shall have his freedom. I proclaim't.

Cop.   How can it
Avail, save to exasperate the South?

Lin.   With charity to all, and with malice
Toward none, an unswerving march toward
The right, we purpose to keep on without
Respect to sympathies or schemes, or snares,
Or overtures with wrong. An upright course
Alone remains to honor.

Cop.   Peace, peace! It is the cry. Peace at any
Cost; on any terms; swap of sentiments;
Change of banners; anything to stanch this
Flow of blood.

Lin.   Never swap horses while you ford a stream.
It has gone forth. The bondsman shall be free.
It may prove even so; and its effect
Like the Pope's bull against the comet. No
Mortal knows. I govern not events.; they govern
Me. The jarring household trembles. Why? Can
A house against itself divided, stand?
How reads the precept? I am convinced that
With the house divided, we are lost—and
Liberty. I am but human, therefore,
Am liable to err. I would restore
The Union; would perform the dictates of
A mind impressed with a keen sense of right
And freedom to all men; converting
The vile dogma that "might makes right", to right
Makes might; and through the pathless billows of
This motto, guide the ship of State.

Cop.   [*Aside.*] Confound him! Too honest con-
       descension.
Sir, your argument is well backed; but 'twill not
Give us peace. 'Twill open broad the blood-gates!
A wild lay of the winding-sheet! You quote
The Counsellor; but the same said also,
"Blest are the peace-makers".

LIN. But shall I cast your pearls before the
    swine?

COP. I'd cede them territory, freedom, all;
If I could but procure the boon of peace
We crave.

LIN. Conceed the South all claims, give them
    secession?

COP. I would do anything to hasten peace.

LIN. Well, then it must be said we disagree.
And further; to be candid, think you your
Heart is right? A traitor to your country!
Shame! Your follies would disintegrate all ties
Of public strength and end in degrading
You. Preposterous!

COP. State rights, State sovereignty! Liberty!
It is this glorious principle which I
Defend. Those States have sacred rights, which if
Denied, or ravished, hurl their material
Consequences, in desolating war,
Back upon their dictatorial foe!

LIN. I cannot lengthen this discussion.
Only say the wrong don't fester here; but
In the blight of bondage. No sovereignty
On earth has rights to hold its people slaves.
Your power-disintegrating plans are green of venom.
A good day.   [*Exit* LINCOLN.

COP. I've incurred his ire and I do fear that
I shall be arrested.

Re-enter THUG.

BILL. Its dangerous to stay in the country. I'm
going to Canada. Hark! Did you hear that gun?
I tell you it isn't safe. I expect they'll burn all
the houses and kill everybody they catch. If I
should be caught, I presume I should be hanged by
the great toes, head downward. A half million men
armed with horrid weapons to the teeth! Oh, I do

wish you had convinced him and persuaded him to
make peace.

THUG.   Hanged by the toes did 'e say?
What signifies such hanging?   Why they'll hang
Him by the gambrels with a thong.
With hemp, gnarl-knotted in his hair, they'll stretch
Him horizontal; face, sun-ward; eyelids
Cropped; eyeballs ashoot; corpus adingle
Dangle forty feet above a hungry
Ditch dug two by six.   Why, Val, his legs 'twixt
Two sour apple trees, straddled apart, with
Twisted cords they'll yank, till the blood oozes
Up to a parting-pitch.   He'll flop shrieking,
A naked, sun-bak'd coward!   Why, they'll blow
Burnt powder from a million firelocks in
His skin;   bang him with mock shrapnel and hand
Grenades !   They'll use his shirt for wads;   shrivel
Him up by pellets and indian arrow
Heads.   Bah !   How they'll howl and grin and
      grimace
At his odd, quivering quirks, squeals, squeaks and
Squalls !   Die like a man?   Aye, that's delicious
Dying !   Be martyred to the valiant cause
Of cowards, for if their powder-blazes
Don't finish him, the sun and buzzards will.

  BILL. Canada, Canada !   Straight for Canada !
  THUG. Well blubbered.   See that ye buffet safe the
Floods of old Saint Lawrence.   The biggest sharks
That lumber round that baby gulf-stream are
Yankee land-sharks.   You'll make a muckle dish
For two, for they've a bounty on weak scalps
And go for every timid sucker
Finning nor'ward.   Right delicate game to
Munch and crunch !   The lubber has a tooth for
Bounties and bounty-jumpers;   a hungry
Throat, thick set, like a holly hedge, with guns

And jav'lins. You'll make a dish of sweetmeats.
You're a mulish maukin. The South can slough
You off; and you're not wanted here; better
Be the angle of a shark. [*Aside.*] See him slide
Backward, like a crawfish! [*Exit* BILL.

Cop. No wonder Pet, the wretched creature's
    scared.
Oh when I think of the enormous debt
Accumulating, the carnage and the
Misery, the devastation, disgrace,
Confusion and mockery of other
Nations, the groveling humility
And the list of horrors this war entails!

Thug. And you were won
Completely over by that morpion,
Who has no common sense; and very much
Resembles a circus clown.

Cop. Don't say that. I had a fearless combat
With his Excellency, and argued peace.

Thug. It is not peace I want. Revenge and its
Reward! I'm off. Good day, I'm busy with
A scheme. [*Aside.*] Excellency! [*Exeunt omnes.*

    Re-enter LINCOLN *musing.*

Lin. The hour hangs dark and gloomy. Doubts
    and fears
Beset my path, and the thorns of sorrow,
Censure, malice, bed their lengths into my
Being. My darken'd soul, canst not dispel
This gloom! Oh! 'tis a fearful pall that shades
        [*The horizon gradually darkens.*
My heart. 'Twould seem the skinny webs
Of dismal saurians are flapping through
Atmospheres of fog, while hissing serpents
Crawl beneath and gnash their fangs; gather and
Dart at good. Armies of locusts wither
Justice. Worms prey on windrows of the slain.

Toads, centipedes, scorpions throng the ways,
While sultry dragons flit the moral air
And vitiate all that's pure.   Virtue seems seized
With paroxysmal throes and begets fiends,
Who band in offensive squadrons against
Liberty.   Charity is purblind to
The monstrousness of evil; hope, the last
Resource of my spirit, beaming fainter,
Enthusiasm flies.   And yet, I pause:
From the far fields of Vicksburg, welcome wave
The tidings of grand achievements fledging
Into fact.   Heaven blandly smiled in granting
Us one Grant to freedom's weal; and in that
Grant I'll fix my faith.   'Tis an expanse of
Military tact, that flanks and winds and
Disconcerts a foe so arch as this.   In
Good designs we'll trust and onward toil, no
Longer lingering in hesitation,
But steadfast plod our progress through, till blest
With victory.

SCENE II.   *The battle ground of* GETTYSBURG.
*Heavy firing.   Rebel and Federal soldiers pass across
the stage, skirmishing.*

Enter several Sharp-shooters.

FIRST SHARP.   Pick the officers Sam.   Hit's no
use wastin' bullets on common fellers, while thar's
any uv the big shoulder-strappers.   This h'yer's a
rich kentry.   Look at this piece uv sile; see me jest
wring the grease right out on't; hit's that fat.

SECOND SHARP.   Yis, we'd a hed a mighty soft
march out h'yer, ef our officers hed'nt been so awful feard uv hurtin' somebody.   Gals, any 'mount
on em; an' did ye notice how wite an' purty they
be?

THIRD SHARP.   I noticed hit, an' thar's another

thing I noted, wot is, thet ye don't see among 'em
any uv that ar coward, copperhead natur ye see in
the men.   They're either full blooded Yank or full
blooded Sesesh.   Sich gals is gals.   They haint no
skulks.   I got a nat'ral animosity agin' them nuthern copperheads.   They're skulkin' varmints b'lorg-
in' ter the snake race; but the women's a superior
article.

FIRST SHARP.   An' cf our gin'rals war'nt so confounded purtic'lar, we mought uv every one on us
a hed a honsome gal an' all the gold an' greenbacks
we could kerry hum.

Enter Federal officers; Gen. REYNOLDS, *on
horseback, giving orders.*

SECOND SHARP.   Hold on, boys, see.   H'yer's
game fur yer powder.   Hide yeuw, right smart behine yen hedge an' be ready.   I'm a goin' to climb
up this h'yer tree an' squat in the leaves.   Thet
ar's a gin'ral.   He's my game.   Boys, pick yer men.
I take thet feller on the hoss.

THIRD. SHARP.   Yis, I reckon hit costs ye yer life.

SECOND SHARP.   Th'et's nothin'.

OFFICER.   General, the battle seems focusing
To the right.   The enemy is gath'ring
In the valley with obvious intent
To storm the circling ridges and allure
Us into stratagem.

REYNOLDS.   [*Surveying with field-glass.*]   I will
Arrange my whole division, thus: The first.....

[*Report of Sharp-shooter's rifle.*   REYNOLDS *falls.*
Its over with me!

OFF.   Oh, he is killed!

[*He sinks into the arms of Officers,*
REYN.   Stand by the flag, soldiers.   [*Dies.*
JOE *steps forward, aims and fires.   Sharp-shooter
falls.   Officers bear the General's body off the field.*

Cannonading hushed. Curtain falls, but rises, representing the battle of the second day.

Enter Gen. MEADE. *Staff following.* FLORENCE *attending the wounded.*

MEADE. The armies are coming to a mighty
Action. To-day will be most memorable.
We must put forth our utmost energies
To check the rebels' fierce intention of
Forcing a position on the heights.

Enter BOB, *as Courier.*

BOB. Gen'ral, the Rebs have driven us from a
Portion of the ridge. Our men are frantic
For the onset; while our corps commander
Dallies for orders from their head.

MEADE. [*Writing*] Here, bear with haste, this
    message to him. My
Order is: be cool and steadfast. [*Exit* BOB.

Enter second courier.

SECOND COUR. General, the hero of the line I
Represent, sends, in great haste for orders.
The lines are vascillating from the shock
The enemy hurl against us.

Enter dispatch bearers.

MEADE. Rush these dispatches to the officers.
The contest waxes bloody, yet 'twill rest
Unfinished till to-morrow. Great action
Must be made; great energy and coolness,
Courage indomitable and careful
Management of commands. Bid them deceive.
Harass, frustrate and plague the enemy. [*Exit
courier.*] Officers, this is the culminating
Struggle of the rebellion. If we do
Our duty, ere the sun hides his crimson
Colors in the west, he'll view the proudest

Conflict the world e'er witnessed, done.
'I he grandest theme discussed, the vict'ry won.

[*Exeunt omnes.*

SCENE III. *Idem.*

Third day. A rocky height. Skirmishing.

Enter squads of the Buck-tails. COL. TAY-
LOR *at their head. The enemy in occupation of the
height. Din of battle heard, and rebel yell.*

COL. Push on brave boys, they slowly yield.
Our heroism wins the field.
The duel of artillery,
The madden'd rush of cavalry,
The hundred thousand muskets' rattle,
All the wild tempest of the battle
Quiver and dally on the poise.
Your brunt must overbalance, boys.
Charge once more the blazing height!
Charge with bayonets, left and right!
Through minnies' shriek, through deaf'ning yells,
Through murd'rous storms of shot and shells,

Enter JOE *with* QUASH *and colored troops.*

Follow your leader! Ah, I'm hurt;
'Tis but a scratch. On! Don't desert
Your post of honor.—— Ah, a haze
Steals on my vision. Luckless maze
To blind me now! [*Sinks. Friends cluster round.*
Goes well the battle?

CAPT. Oh, he is dying. Our noble Colonel!

JOE. Boys, is yer Cunnel killed? Rush fur 'em,
men, the Rebs is givin' way. We'll git scalpish
vengeance fur that ar. H'yer, Gray-back; yo the
crotch-pole as killed the Cunnel?

SHARP-SHOOTER. Say, yeuw. I'm gin orders fur
te pick the officers, wot I'm pullen' at right smart;
but I'm darned ef I kin make out whe'rr yeuw'm an

officer ur a sawmill, fur te waste a feller's ammer-
nition onto. Say, yeuw, what's hit ye call yerself?
A ring-tailed roarer, or a rip-snorter?

JOE. I don't gin'rally wait ter be called, when
thar's a fight agoin'. I'm a thinkin' whuther ter
skin yer alive, or hamstring ye like I would arry a
wild rooter; but bein' as ye're the sneakin' traitor
wot shot his betters, like a coward a crawlin' about
the grass, I've made up my mind fur ter slit yer jug-
'lar fust.

SHARP. Wal, I've no purtic'lar objections to a
game uv hash.

JOE. All right; ye'll 'tarnal quick git fixed out,
that a'way. [*They fight with bowies.*] Charge on
'em, com'erds, I'll be thar soon as I immerlate this
h'yer wolf-eater. Thar, d'ye want any more?

SHARP. Oeough! Ye've stuck me. Hev I come
all the road from Tex te fine my match with bowies?
He, ho, ye've run it deep! Bones uv a spook! Let
me cuss ye, 'fore I die.   [FLORENCE
      approaches the death scene.

      Enter Surgeons.

Ther's no use fur ye, gal, I'm past medicine. Tell
'em ter bury me whar I fell. Hit's honorablest; an'
keep tham nuthern sugeons away from me. I hed
a heart wonst, afore thet hell-cat ripped it out uv
me. H'yer, gal, send this yer hum ter Texas.
[*Gives her a package.*] Wat'll my own putty pets
do? I feel the tow-cord uv my life ontwistin'; goin', goin'! Poor darlin' wife an' babies; farewell;
an' my good old mother, I bless ye all. H'yer,
yank, take my fresh cusses. Devils gnaw ye! Devils gnaw ye!   [*Dies.*

JOE. I never made a motion I was'nt sorry fur.
Fiddle, fiddle! Am I a baby? No time fur senta-
munts. H'yer's no place fur ter onbottle yer brine,

gal, go whar I haint been an ye'll find somebody
half hit. [*Aside.*] I must quit sight uv that ar gal.
She puts me in mind uv my mother. I seed that ar
same ghost uv a ministrin' angel wonst afore; she
takes the varmint killin' wrath right out uv me. I
confess I've a right smart uv a likin' fur her; but
'taint the love uv a loveyer. Charge on em, men!
[Exeunt Joe and soldiers.

Enter a Herald.

Her. Ho, joyful tidings!
Col. [*Rousing.*] What? What's the fortune
   of the day? Is the
Field ours?
Her. The heights are captured. The enemy is
Yielding, slow and doggedly.

Enter Second Herald.

Second Her. The columns of the foe are bro-
   ken. Whole
Regiments come forward and surrender.
[Shouting without.
Meade. The field that costs us two score thou-
   sand lives,
Is won. Vict'ry has perched upon our banners.
[Shouts of victory on all sides.
Col. Now let me die! Oh, word of victory!
That thrilleth my pulseless nature! Welcome,
Welcome my death, with victory.   [*Dies.*

Enter a Messenger.

Mess. If I should say a hundred thousand slain,
'Twould sound incredible; yet num'bring all,
Disabled, dead, and every way thrown *hors*
De combat, on both sides, it could not fall
Far short. The ears are tortured with the groans
Of dying warriors; and sadness drapes this
Vale of victory. The goal, the welcome

Goal our anxious hope long coveted, has
Ilove in view.   It stands enshrined in the sky;
Muffled in clouds, like nebulæ which spot
Its disc; and yet, dim as its lustre, 'tis
A luminary bearing such mellow
And enchanting influence, that the righteous
Thrill with an exuberance of joy and
Shout, hail Liberty!   Thou sweetest boon of
Life.   Welcome, with thy exhilarating
Smiles and light our swelling bosoms.
For thee, we fight and bleed and die.

Scene IV.   *Idem.*

A company of colored soldiers.   QUASH, *as Captain.*

QUASH.   Say, Jambo, we's jes did some bustin'
big shootin' an' guess ole mars'll shet to lickin' us,
now.   Heah, heah.   Dis yer's de fall ob de great
Babylon, de wicked harlot ob de rebelations. [*Sings.*

"Don't you see de black clouds
      Risin' ober yonder,
Whar de massa's ole plantation am?
      Nebber you be frightened—
      Dem is orly darkies,
Come to jine an' fight for Uncle Sam.

ALL IN CHORUS.

"Look out dar, now!
      We's a gwine to shoot!
Look out dar—don't you understand?
      Babylon is fallen!
      Babylon is fallen!
And we's a gwine to occupy de land.

"Don't you see de lightnin'
      Flashin' in de canebrake,
Like as if we gwine to hab a storm?
      No! you is mistaken—

'Tis de darkey's bay'nets,
An' de buttons on dar uniform.

Chorus.

"Way up in de corn-field,
  Whar you hear de tunder,
Dat is our ole forty pounder gun;
  When de shells is missin',
  Den we load wid punkins,
All de same to make de cowards run."

Chorus.

Enter Messenger.

Mess.   To all the world proclaim,
Heaven is propitious!   The joyful news
Of the capitulation of the great
Strong-hold of Vicksburg, comes on the arrow
Head of lightning; official from Gen'ral
Grant, commanding.   'Tis confirmed!   A city,
A hundred cannon and a defiant
Force of thirty thousand veterans!

Enter Custer, *Commander of Horse.*

Cust.   Now, have the jolly chords of freedom
      struck
A tintinabulation; and grateful
Harmony dispels the tones of discord.
What!   In so brief a space, all auspices
Upturned?   That which but now was doubt and
      gloom
Changed to cheery brightness?   Decrees reversed
Their meaning?   Gruff verdicts of disaster
Wheeled into triumphs?   Aye, and the storm
Clouds which were wont to pour drenching torrents,
Vanish from the sky!   The ocean billows
That to-day, heaved, swelled and gaped their crater

Jaws, swallowing with devouring glutt'ny
The noblest votaries of freedom, are,
Of a sudden, calmed.   That was, is not; that
Ceased to be expected, comes copiously.
For the bright sun of liberty, long dimmed
By veils of unsuccess, rises in crimson;—
Tinges of sympathetic agony—
And as he views the tide of battle turned,
Unmasks his glories; and our thankful hearts
By his resplendent beams afresh illumed,
Beat joyfully in concert with shouts of
Hail, mightiest Chieftain!   Heaven hath smiled
Propitious, on thy prophetic mandate:
The great Proclamation ushered to the
Lowly bondsman!   Thy intrepid nerve, through
Opposition barred and bolted, gnashing
Anger, polluting calumnies, blasphemous
Threats of fiends oppugnant, hath triumphed!   **Two**
Vict'ries in a day!   One drives the shafts of
Terror home to the heart of treachery
At the East, the other blots his prospects
In the West.   [*Exit.*

SCENE V.   *A plantation near Vicksburg.*
      Slaves at work in the cotton field.

FIRST SLAVE.   Say, Smokey, how long'll I be a
git'n ober dar to weah dat good news am?

SECOND SLAVE.   Dat ar 'pends altogedder on cir-
cumstances, sah.   If you goes afoot 't'l take about
an houah; if you goes on de mule, take 'bout a half
an houah; but if you goes aboard o' one ob dese yer
new-fangle smoke wagons, most deyah now.

FIRST SLAVE.   Josh, did you note as how dem
big Yankee guns is stop firin'?

THIRD SLAVE.   Ya, he, dat's putty talk, wen ebery body know dat.   Look'eah, Quim, dat news am

jolly.   I's gwine to cut loose out ob workin' foh de
boss widout pay.   Dis yer slab'ry's a humbug.   We's
free.   We's gwine to rank in de fust quality.   [*Sings.*

"Say darkey, hab you seen my massa
    Wid de muftache on his face ?
Go 'long de road sometime dis mornin'
    Like he's gwine to leab de place.
He seen de smoke way up de ribber,
    Whar de Linkum gum boats lay,
He took his hat an' left putty sudden
    An' I specs he's runned away.

ALL IN CHORUS.

"De Massa run, ha, ha!
    De darkey stay, ho, ho !
It must be now dat de kingdom's comin'
    An' de year ob jubilo,

"He's six foot one way an' two foot tudder,
    An' he weighs tree hundred poun'.
His coat so big dat he couldn't pay de tailor,
    An' it wont go half way roun'.
He drills so much dey call 'im Cap'n,
    An' he gets so drefful tanned
I spec he's a gwine to fool dem yankees
    For dey tink he's a contraband.

CHORUS.

"De darkeys dey'll get lonesome libin'
    In de log cabin on de lawn
Dey move dey're tings into massa's parlor
    For to keep it while he's gone,
Dar's wine an' cider in de kitchen
    An' de darkeys dey'll hab some,
For I spec 'twill all be cornfiscated,
    When de Linkum sojers come".

ACT V.

Scene I. Richmond.   *A secret vault of a prison. Enter Cop, as janitor.*

Cop.   Well done!   I have been wond'rous successful
In this rôle of two games at a time.
I've an opinion, watching the wav'ring
Motions of this war, the average squabbling
Surges liveliest against the South. Now,
Spirits like mine, hell-bound to be winners,
Souls which have no predilection, and whose
Joys at the tumble-down of either, do
Best find vent in hidden chuckle, loving
To court pleasure out of both wrecks, must
Hazard some dangerous contiguity
Which show most misery from dividing
Lines of contest. Ha, ha, ha! Revenge and
Curiosity! A right dismal pair
Of twin impulses—inspiring one 'bove
Danger's terrors, push one into many
A grim adventure. Aye, apt expedient
Outwits detection! Why, I'm a hit at
Games of make-believe; and can crack cunning
Quirks. Ain't I a politician? From Bull
Run bomb-blasts, to Federal bombast—all
The way through Dry Tortuga-torture, through
Qui-vives of conscription, even to this
Subterranean-den of the assassin,
Whither I hold the keys of entrance. Ha!
I've lived so long, I'm waxing short, and 'twere
A wonder I am here, did not my length
And shortness bring me—length of life's ennium
Paucity of corporeal measure;

For conscription it means slaughter; and the
Slaughter's common to all men, these days. Then
'Tis to Messrs Longevity and Decrepitude
I owe my life; to whom am I indebted
For this situation? Let's see : to a
White man? There's no such biped left. Pedals
There be for locomotion; but at heart,
White men have vanished from the earth. I
Judge humanity from men's regard of
Me. But, mum. I'm getting to distrust the
Silence of the grave. Well, 'tis time for
Their arrival. The plot. The plot. Boozy;
Slipped my mind; oh, yes,—my situation.
I owe it to the slave. Query. How so?
A slave is troubled with a slippery tongue.
'Twont do to talk your plans and plots before
Him. Some even credit him with mind to
To con surmises. So much the worse for
Him and good for superannuated
Pedagogues, green as the hill slopes of their
Decadence; and simple as the dotage
In their limp. I'm royalty's worshiper—
Got up for an occasion—improvised
Out of the remnants of a public man
Made private through Abe Lincoln's ostracism.
Ha, ha! A situation got by sworn
Pledges of loyalty to the king. Oh,
How loyal! I do love my sovereign!
    [Enter THUG, *stealthily, with a pick-lock.*
Honors me with his precious confidence,
In trusting his wig-made aged teacher
With this key of hell. Oh, most generous
And noble sovereign! He, he, he, he!
Pay in Confed'rate scrip. It is my bread and
Butter; black bread, you know—the color of
His temper. So I'll thank longevity

And decrepitude for life, liberty
And the pursuit of happiness.

    THUG.   [*Aside.*]   You old villain,
I much suspect this loyalty you prate.

    COP.   Ho, ho, 'tis best to be merry
            When you wouldn't be sad.
            Whack fal de rol. Derry,
            Old rye and sweet sherry
            Are beautiful very
            And make the heart glad.
                           I know
Where the keys to the vintage are kept.
                    [*Capers while* THUG *talks.*

    THUG.   [*Aside.*]   You worthless old dandy; I've
    a mind to
Carve you. No—poor policy. Hypocrite
And Turk! Yet I'll make him serve some lively
Purpose ere this meeting closes. A song,
Or dance will give them fresher spirits if
Their purpose flag; and then, see?—a gentle
Rupture of the villian's skin with this, will
Circumvent his babble.   [*Exit* THUG, *unnoticed.*

    COP.   Aye, a great success!
Powder, dungeon, draft, banishment, hangdog's
Halter—outdone, for vengeance sake. Hold! Here
They come, tiptoe! Timid of wine's nightmare.
Genius meus, thou shalt yet conjure strokes
Of twisted meaning and cram the itch-fires
Of a great crime's superstition with the
Hyena food of mad infatuation;
Since I foresee their cause is lost! And ere
The fall, the thug must do his deed   [*Knocking.*

    Janitor opens the door. Re-enter THUG, *with*
DAVIS, WINDER, BRECKENRIDGE, SURRAT *and others.*

    DAVIS.   The small hour of time's ominous pointer!
At this dark vigil, with this risky task,

In caverns of an Elk, which never
Knew a sunbeam, one trembles at the grate of
Rusty hinges. The turfy floor quivers
Like a scum that films the yawning fissures
Of perdition. What! A festivity!

[DAVIS *waves the janitor out.*

[*To* THUG.] Well, thou hast come on my demand
    to make
A finish of the contract.

THUG. Touching commissions for security
And the compensation.

DAVIS. I'll produce commissions for as many
As thou shalt see fit to enter in thy
Gang; But as to money....

THUG. Faugh! Nonsense, sir. Think'st thou
Assassins go unpaid?

DAVIS. As leader of a band that kill the President,
His Cabinet and Generals, what gold
Is thy demand?

THUG. One million.

DAVIS. 'Tis too much.

THUG. Thou asked'st my demand; I gave it
Thee. One million. gold.

DAVIS. I'll say the half of it.

THUG. I take no fractions. 'Tis not a job
Which limiteth of division. Suppose that I
And my accomplices, should halve this work
Ye order; and murder half these tyrants
On the list; leaving the other half to
Wriggle like maggots, into the rotten
Offal of dead men's power; and with the
License following sudden rise, they dart
A ruthless, ill-dissembled rage upon
Thy head!

DAVIS. No, no; 'twont do. We mean to have
    them all

Wiped from the eyries of the earth. We mean
That at daybreak after the extirping—
Their leaders, all defunct—a chaos never
Known of human governments, shall hover
Pulselessly; decked in the shrouds of horror
Indecision and despair, athwart their
Wretched city. Their great metropolis
Shall gurgle through its million aqueducts,
In lieu of the now crystal waters, a
Griping hemlock; which tasted, nor old nor
Young, rich, poor, male, female, white, black, states-
    man.
Philosopher, priest nor physician e'er
Sparred the subtle hug of his quietus.
We mean contagion, pestilence, gunpowder
Plots, conflagrations, and every scourge of
The destroying angel shall stalk
Abroad and drive their stiffening stings into
The flesh of our defiant adversary,
In the subversion of their arrogance;
The execution of which terrible
Commission we have reserved for thee.
    THUG.   Aye, thy commission would I execute.
Already I've schooled a dozen daring
Spirits to the enterprise; and I have
Planted deep the seed of this my plotting,
To destroy thine enemies. But in the
Sad contingent of thy parsimony,
I'll winnow to the winds my darling scheme
And thou that wouldst a monarch live, canst die
A slave.
    DAVIS.   Nonsense sir, I'll have't not so. Thou
    canst have
Whate'er be thy demand. Descend, now, to
Thy knee, before thy liege, and thou shalt rise
A knight. Arise, take thy commission as

A Colonel; and here are the commissions
For the conspirators thou designated'st
As safe-guards, in case of apprehension.
    THUG. Thanks, thanks, my liege; but what of
      the reward?
    DAVIS. I grant a full appropriation of
The sum required to meet expenses, and
To thee in case thou executest well
Thy dangerous task, I grant thy million.
    THUG. Good; yet, most gracious sov'reign, in
      summing
This so amicable compact, wilt not
Refuse to yield thy benediction on
Its swift outcome.
    DAVIS. [*Aside.*] The fellow's zeal doth make me
      shudder! How
Can I bless this horrid crunching of
The innocent, by yonder blacken'd wretch?
Hypocracy, perdition! Yet 'tis
Congruous unto repudiation—
The fundament of my philosophy.
    THUG. [*Aside.*] See, they recoil; but I must
      have an oath.
A plastic superstition doth pervade,
Which fixeth my intentions. This oath shall
Be my oracle. [*Aloud.*] Where is yon turnkey?
    ALL. No!
    THUG. He is a funny elf; can dance and sing,
My lords, this nightly convocation weigh'th
Upon ye; whereas the daylight giveth
Vigor. 'Twas a mischance that we adopted
Night for this dark business; for bravado
Best strutteth like a pavo, in the eye
Of noon; and as the eve approacheth—his
Bombast shadow'd by the light's decline—
Mark him cower unto his roost of safety!

ALL.   Ha! Are we cowards?

DAVIS.   What, fellow ?   Questionest thou our daring?

THUG.   There's no credit due the poor assassin,
Whose work is done at night.   Ho, janitor!

ALL,   'Twill never do!

THUG.   Leave just this thing to me.   My lords,
I know
Your man too well to think him capable
Of our betrayal.   His tongue shall never

Re-enter Janitor.

Blab.   Say, my good veteran, bring hither
Wine, sir, for all this company, thyself
Included.

DAVIS.   Do as he bids thee, sirrah.

COP.   [*Aside.*]   Ah, ha, I know that fellow; just
from the
Enemy!   Thug.   I'll be bound he knows me,
Too; but does not recognize me.   Zounds! but I
Must draw close my old disguise for safety.
Not that I feel surprise.   What am I here
For?   Is't not to coquette with the weasel
I am hawking and carry off the booty?
But the fellow has a wicked look and
Cynic sneer that wither and appall.

[*Brings wine-glasses and is busy.*

THUG.   Is thy name Fox ?   Here, Foxy, my good
friend,
Canst thou dance ?   I've a partiality to
Dancers.   Thou hast a rosy face and mirth
Dwells in thy twinkle.   Come, friends, doff this
Stateliness.   Ho, for a spree on equal
Footing!   I'll pour the wine.   Come, Foxy, drink
To the king.

COP.   That will I.   So here's prosper thy prospects,
My sovereign liege !   [*All are irrepressibly won by*

the assassin's management and henceforth allow him
his full caprice.]

THUG. Great! Thou shalt be toast giver. Fox,
 my boy,   [*Pouring a second bout.*]
Wine is my bev'rage. Good my lords, another
Round! Now, man, what for the generals?

COP. The gen'rals of this nation! Wide con-
 quests,
Great victories, long lives, fair ladies and
Immortal names.   [*Cheers.*

THUG. Well, what now for the lords and statesmen?   [*Pours third round.*

COP. The Lords and Statesmen to his Majesty!
May they so counsel and administer,
That from the wreck of conquest, a mighty
Empire rise, which nursed by aliment of
My sov'reign's judgment shall bloom and flourish
Ever.   [*Cheers.*

THUG. Fox, thou'rt a genius or a king's fool; and
The gist of the one includes the meaning
Of the other. But what about a dance?

JAN. My Liege and Lords, when I was pedagogue
No doubt my legs were nimble; but old age,
The same unwelcome thief that stole my power
To battle for my country, hath stol'n my
Sprightliness. But good my lords, as I'd not
Wish to ruffle your desires, will tender
Just one fraction of the skill I once possessed;
Less perfect, as the proportion of the
Laggard sloth, to the agility of the
Nimble cat.   [*Dances to music.*

ALL. Bravo, bravo. A song, a song!

DAVIS. Give us a song, old boy, thy wit would
 flurry
Wizzards. Thou'rt a king's fool indeed.
We'd have a premonitory song from thee,

And let it appropriate to this occasion be.

Enter FLORENCE, *half visible, robed in spectral white. She kneels in a sombre part of the room, unnoticed by all, except* DAVIS *and* COP.

COP.   SONG.

I rescued her from a frowning grave
I snatched her out of its yawning cave;
When neither the king nor his soldiers brave
 Could aught but to pall at her shriek.
She stood like a lily, though crimson clad,
With its petals unfolded, in tears so sad;
For her warriors, brave warriors, faint, wound-
  ed and dead,
 Lay helpless and cold at her feet.

She writhed in an agony, agony rare
Her vesture disheveled, her proud head bare,
Rude winds swept her tresses of golden hair
 And adversity flaunted and mocked,
When I, groaning with pity, afar off stood,
Conceived that to *silence the conquering brood,*
Might free this fair lady of sorrowful mood,
 Of the griefs that around her had flocked.

THUG. Old Fox, thy song is more ominous than tangible. Thou art, a prophet and a king's fool; as thy cleverness will testify. Thou art also a witch's mate, as thy auguries show. Canst give us a touch of witchcraft? [*Pours fourth round.*] My lords Sure, these are old baronial days returned.
A wizzard's fox; [*Aside.*] rather, a deep dyed spy!
Here, Fox, drink me a dainty sentiment;
Poor me, the humblest of them all.
 COP. Adventurous youth, here's that the en-
  terprise,
 So deeply planned,

Meet on its gold alluring skies
   No hindering hand.
  DAVIS. [*Rising*] What meanest thou, wizzard?
   Tell me, is not
This the turnkey? What's this he seem'th to smell?
  COP. Ye call me wizzard. I am;—a friendly
Witch's mate, with auguries refined.
  THUG. Drink, my lords. I like his sentiments.
                      [*They all drink.*
Now for an augury. Let us hear the
Wild, mysterious wisdom of a fortune
Teller.
  COP.   My lords,

I'll mix a compound of your several wishes;
   And ye shall quaff it in the toast of wine;
For if ye do this with the touch of dishes
   And pledge of constancy, [*To* THUG,] suc-
      cess is thine.

  THUG. Most delightful! We'll have it so. [*Aside.*
The rascal; he has deciphered me! Most
Likely he's a spy. I shall destroy him.
Repudiator has got wondrous quiet.
            [DAVIS *is staring at* FLORENCE.
Ah, keep cool. How wiz enjoys it, see!
Well, I use him to accomplish my designs.
[*Aloud.*] I like it, Wizzy; it suits well. Go on.

  COP. Now, good my lords, I must demand,
    With pardon for so bold a stand,
    That ye each write your pressing wish,
      Couched in your fewest cogent words.
    Each one, upon a paper slip,
    I'll close my sight and dream a bit.
    Then, as your slave, interpret it
      With this aruspic darm of birds.

THUG.   Cheer, e'en in the sham that apeth merriment!
Well done, my faithful wizzard.   What stroke of
Sorcery hath now possessed thee?
COP.   [*Holding up his vials.*] My Liege, in this
talismanic compound
I'm informed of the fortunes, good or bad,
Of your adventure.
THUG.   What adventure?   What knowest thou
of an adventure?
COP. I speak in allegory, as a liegeman, inspired.
ALL.   Agreed! [*They write and deliver the slips.*
COP.   [*Pompously.*]
'Tis the joy of the sorcerer ever to show
To a cloud covered mind all the truth it may know.
            Breathing soft invocation
            We mix this oblation;
Lo, a weird incantation will presently flow!

Already conceiveth the matrical wine
And the embryo forms, as they grow, we divine.
            There's a crone, old and haggard.
            Ha, Thug, girt and daggered,
Yon gaunt, lank and laggard old tyrant is thine.

My lords, let us drink the red draught to its lees.
'Tis a wish full of vengeance; lisps hateful decrees.
            Would ye have that wish granted?
            Drink the seed ye have planted,
That your visions enchanted grow fact by degrees.

            [*To* THUG.]   May the monarch with his blessing, the drug, the weapon and the
genii of all shrines lend you God speed!
DAVIS.   [*Giving a purse to the assassin.*] And
this my pledge of constancy and protection and my
blessing upon thee, and thy undertaking, shall ever
be kept most sacred.

THUG. Enough, enough, gracious liege, I'm con-
tent. [*Pours fifth round with much ceremo-
ny. All drink the last bout amidst jubilee.
Exit* COP, *running, and re-enters, staggering.*
ALL. Gracious God!
DAVIS. · [*To Thug.*] What hast thou committed?
THUG. Nothing at all, my liege, nothing at all;
I say nothing; well, 'twas a stingy deed;—
I have exiled him. 'Twas plain to me the
Climate here, were too unsteady for an
Instrument so delicate and I've transferred him
To a warmer sphere. Hush, no praises, friends,
A pigmy favor 'twas, I rendered you.
Know ye 'tis no sin to kill a wizzard!
It he who kills can waive the furies' spell,
The penalty is honor. [*To* COP.] I know thee,
I know thee, blatant copperhead! Banished
For treason from thy native land, in that
Thou bragged'st secession, played'st the spy and by
Thy perfidy puttest thy friends to blush.
Off with that grizzly wig and show thy years,
Thou menial! [THUG *tears off his disguise and the
Janitor attempts to escape but is prevented.*
COP. I pray you let me hence; for I am ill.
T'G. And thou'lt be better soon, worse sooner, but
Soonest, a quaking mass of fear; for I
Have poisoned thee! Ha, ha, thou withy knave!
What, shuddering at the news? Thou'lt have to
Blubber fast thy witchcraft; and thy rhyming
Eloquence must wax more voluble, or
'Twill not all spin out. He, he, he!
COP. Shades of all horrors, I am dying! My
Vitals feel the grip of the unwelcome
Monster. Help, help me! What, murderer! What
Tempted thee to this? Oh, death! Thou'rt all
Unwelcome! My voice grows hoarse and husky—
Soul—hap—less—gnarl—self-re—proach! [*Dies.*

SCENE II. *Union camp, before Richmond.*

Enter QUASH, *at the head of colored squad.*

QUASH. Left, right, left, right, left, right, halt! Right about, face. File off, outposts, boaf sides ob de tent, right an' left. De fust man dat budges a foot from de place git fifty ball troo 'is body.

COLORED PICKET. Woeah! dat's mighty tall talk to be pwoclaimin' to gemmen, what's as nigh on to git'n dar fweedom as we is.

QUASH. Grant's bwung up a half a million sogers. I's commissioned to 'splode de mine gwine un'er de city an' blow up Jeff. Davis an' de whole rebel crew.

SOLDIER. Ya, dat berifies a passage ob scripture wot I heerd a readin'....

QUASH. Wot am dat passage ob scripture, nig?

SOL. [*Scratching his head.*] Well, I guess I'd 'membered dat if you had'nt 'rupted me.

QUASH. Dat makes out dat if we's gwine to hab discipline, we's gwine to hab discipline, sah. Stay in de ranks, We's officers; we is.

CORPORAL. We's jess boun' to blow 'em up; den we'll hab a gran' jollification. We need'nt cut stick an' run, any more, nuther; foh de fweedom's comin' to us poor darks. We's all gwine to stay an' live on our own plantation. [*Outburst of joy.*

QUASH.   SONG.

We's gwine to hab a 'cidin' battle,
Quah, yah, it's time ole massa gone away,
Away, away, 'cross de sea.
Soon you'll hear de big guns rattle
Whang! Bang! A nigga's touchin' off de fuse ee
Bruise de oberseer ee.

OMNES, IN CHORUS.

Away down souf in Dixie,
　　I'll fight foh de right.
In Dixie's land I'll take my stand,
An' lib an' die in Dixie's land,
Away, away, away down souf, in Dixie.

QUASH.

Come all we darkies, chalk de mark, oh,
Stan' firm, fur Uncle Sammy's pwoclama—
　　Ama—amation make us fwee.
We's gwine to fight an' do our part oh,
'Splode, blow de mines an' parapets away,
　　Away, away to ballygee.

CHORUS.

Away down souf, in Dixie,
　　We's fwee boys. Gig-a-b-hoys!
In Dixie land we take our stand,
We'll lib an' die in Dixie land,
Away, away, away down souf, in Dixie.

QUASH.

Who dat marchin' from de Mississippi?
Who dat comin' from Sabannah city? Dem is Grant
　　An' Sherm' dat beat de Davis pals.
Wha de 'Federates wot'll stan' dar batteries?
Boom! Bomb! an' tunder cannonade to fwee,
　　Me, darkee an' all de gals!

CHORUS.

We fights down souf in Dixie,
　　Hurrah! Huzzah!
An' we's de boys make all dis noise.
Hal'lujah! Spree de jubilee!
Away, away, away down souf in Dixie.

Scene III. RICHMOND. *A room in the Capitol.*

Enter DAVIS *and his secretaries.*

FIRST SEC. Your Excellency, these truths can-
not be
Waived. I urge the danger, since Sherman comes
With legions flushed by vict'ries gained at
Chattanooga, Atlanta, Savannah,
Charleston . . . .

DAVIS. Stop! Don't bore me with such augurs!
All lies
By Jove! All Yankee buncombe!

SECOND SEC. What nonsense! Is truth less truth-
ful for your
Repudiation?

DAVIS. [*Paces.*] Well, grant a part for fact, does't
follow that
Nine tenths is else than gasconade! Have ye
Inspired contagious sanction of reports?
I give no ear to them. I give more thanks
To mutes than babblers.

THIRD SEC. Grant's army like a boa is crawling
Surely and threatens to suffocate us
In its writhing folds. Give ear to reason.

DAVIS. Reason! Out ye driveling sycophants!
Ye shall feed no more upon my bounties.
No concessions, I thunder it! I say
No concessions. Will you heed the baseless
Innuendo! [*Aside.*] Like chilling hailstones they're
Battering 'gainst my heart. Aye they glomerate
Upon my shivering soul and melt not. [*Aloud.*]
Lies all of them, and you the liars. [*Aside.*] And
I'm the chief of liars.— What bugbear's that?

Enter a Messenger.

Mess. Is the President by? I would speak with
Him.

Davis. Well, if you've anything to say, say it.

Mess. I bring a message, sire from General Lee.
He further bids me state that 'tis most useless
To essay a battle.

Davis. [*Tearing it.*] Go tell the coward I repu-
diate
Him as bogus coin. He's flogged the yankees
Plump an hundred times; and now, just in the
Crisis, glory beck'ning at his talent,
His power falls powerless; his bright sword rusts.
Fear unmans him. Go bring his head to me;
And I'll pay thee for't. [*Exit Mess.*] Where are
my gen'rals,
Whose heroic deeds have paralyzed the
World! Oh, Stonewall Jackson, brave, all-con-
qu'ring
Hero! Thy terrors are entombed. Alas;
Wer't thou alive, my cushion were a throne,
My house a palace, and my cap a crown.

Noise without. Re-enter Messenger.

Mess. The cannons roar terrific. 'Tis affirmed
The God of battle yields us the victory.

[*Indistinct cannonading heard.*

'Tis said that Grant in pushing up his troops,
Fell into snares set by the wary Lee;
That he was cut to pieces and half his
Army. The finishing the rest is but
The work of time.

Davis. Man, thou bring'st refreshment to my tired
Soul! Where is he who heralds this report?
Go bring him. If the news prove true, he shall
Be knighted. If false, by heav'n my vengeance
It shall strike the centre of his lying [*Exit Mess.*
Heart and cleave't assunder! What, cannons?

Enter FLORENCE, *dressed as a spy.*

Canst mumble news, sirrah?

FLOR. A slash of the master's sword. A lake of
Gore, a jar of conflict, a wail, and liberty
Is ours. [*Aside.*] 'Tis the liberty thou dreadest,
Tyrant!

DAVIS. Is the news so good? Have our armies
conquered?

FLOR. The news could not be better. Our arms are
Triumphant. [*Aside.*] Ha, villain, thy tyranny
Is at an end. [*Exit* FLORENCE.

DAVIS. Go. I am satisfied. Anxious suspense
Hath gnawed me till the flesh scarce fill'th the gaps
About my bones. With mental torture I'm
So emaciate, that the knocking engine
Of my pulse scarce thobeth its rounds of duty.
But here's an end of toil. Oh, the future!
What a golden prospect! Reclining on
My throne, in wanton dalliance with my thoughts,
I'll take a retrospect. I'll re-endure
These miseries; conjure comparisons
Of past, present and future. The past, a
Vast, tumultuous flood. I, buffeting its
Lurid waves, almost without a compass,
In my bark which but possesseth power to
Buoy me through the tempest; the present, that
Pointeth me to the hav'n of my ambitions;—
Still with a grimace, a convulsion and
A shrug of hateful willingness. Yet, in
The present I behold the city of
My palace; whilst the morn of fortune dawn'th,
All gray and dewy. 'Tis the future! Those
Gilded spires; those sculptured columns, moss-walls;
Symmetric avenues; the elysium!
And yonder golden dome, frowning with kingly
Majesty, grand, massive and forbidding!

O'er *patris manes*, vestas shall hold vigil.
My commons, the jaded slaves! Heading my
Prytanes I'll feast the bloods at the acropolis.
A fit receptacle for potentates like me!

[*Tumult without. Re-enter* FLORENCE.

FLOR. Your Excellencey, fugitives, breathless
Of haste, arrive with tidings of.....
DAVIS. What! Speak, dog! Tidings? What
tidings? That's an
Oily phrase for smirky tyro pedants.
What, does't choke thee? Perk, thou mock'st me
now, with
Hesitation. Speak!
FLOR. Soldiers and other flying harbingers of..
DAVIS. Stop! Vict'ry. and I'll knight thee, b it if
Thou drawl'st 'flying harbingers of overthrow,'
This sword shall thaw thee, frost-numb'd liar, and
Send thy immortal essence to seethe in
Hell! Ah, I unriddle thy device. Thou
Grinn'st the cheer thy lying loth dissembleth!
Watchful anxieties provoke a petulence
Which keen suspense hath frenzied.
FLOR. Your Excellency, if you'll but hear my
words....
DAVIS. Well, bray, now. bray. I listen.
FLOR. 'Twould seem the Union forces are driving
All before them. The confederates are flogged.
A large detachment of the Northern power
Is hurrying hither to take possession.
The battle is enormous. bloody and
Decisive. [*Aside.*] Blanch, quaking wretch, your
crimes
Shall yet be punished! [*Exit* FLORENCE, *followed
by* DAVIS, *sword drawn.*]

Re-enter Messenger and Soldiers.

DAVIS. Grin, dog! Vile traitor! Canst smile
  and twinkle
And spurge thy country's doom upon thy lips?
  MESS. All is lost. Our arms can do no more!
  SOLDIERS. Lost, lost, all hopes are gone!
  FIRST SEC. I warned you of the danger, but
    reckoned
Not the fall so speedy.
  SECOND SEC. Our only hopes be in some grace-
    ful art;
Some sweet conciliation; feign'd innocence;
Some demure submission. 'Tis the only
Artifice we can trump to veer us off
The gibbet. [*Aside.*] But thou, O king! Thou
    hast a
Cause to pale and tremble and fathom down
The depths of thy disaster. Little's the
Pity I bestow, knowing the weight of
Thy egregious guilt. [*Aloud.*] The covenant of
United power must be dissolved by this
Fierce tempest of defeat; and it remain'th
For him who hath a head, to save't as best
He can. That fiendish oath we mumbled,
Fudge! What is it? A meatless nulity.
Old age had shrivled it, ere this last crush.
In youth's prime 'twas strong; and proved a giant
Ghoul which forced us into many a grim
Venture. Now, it culminateth in vast
Discomfiture. I'm ready to renounce
It and forsake its memory.
  THIRD SEC. And I; and curse the day I took it.
  FIRST SEC. And I; for 'twas rot that hath infected
A round million souls.
  DAVIS.   Dust! dust! dust!
  Enter MRS. DAVIS, *attended. She embraces him.*
  MRS. DAVIS. My husband!

DAVIS. Flight! flight!

MRS. DAVIS. Nay, do not say so.

DAVIS. We must fly; it is my only safety.

MRS. DAVIS. But 'twill be disgraceful. The world
will look
Upon us with contempt and we shall be
The butt of ridicule. Prithee do not
Crown this great disaster with disgrace.

DAVIS. What! Woman, wouldst thou have me
hanged? Think'st thou
Of clemency? As though that coarse enemy
At whom I have so often aimed the fury
Of my hatred, would show me tolerance!
Forsaken! Sight thick'neth bleak and eyeballs
Overtask with peering through my courts, to
Find a friend. Even my bosom friend would
See me hanged. Ye vampires! Will none of
You stand forth as volunteers, to guide our
Royal flight?

MRS. DAVIS. Nearest of friends,
Thy being possesseth not the tissues
Which gift the heart of woman, or thy harsh
Crimination had ne'er found utterance.
I would not see thee suffer; and therefore,
Believing escape impossible, I
Wished thee not to undertake it. But if
It best beseem'th thy judgment, I will shame
These parasites, who like poisoning vines,

Enter BRECKENRIDGE.

Feed upon the substance of thy bounty
And now seem ruthlessly deserting thee.
Shame confound their chivalry! In woman's faith
And with confidence in Heav'n, my borrowed
Strength, I undertake the journey; and will
Share thy fortune, my dejected husband,
Though the skies be our pavilion, our camp

Ground the cypress swamp, our evening hymn, the
Doleful moan of caymans, our only breeze.
The fan of bats.   Through the dismal forest,
Echoing with screech of owl and panther,
O'er rivers dreary, the watery, lair of
Serpents, on dim trails of rabid monsters
Which alone track the wild, umbrageous
Wilderness, outside the haunts of man, our
Common enemy, would I fain guide thee
Down to the welcoming ocean; with but
The angels' smile of innocence for our
Palladium, over his rolling billows.

   BRECK.   Lady, thy courage is greater than thy
Strength.   Defeat doth balance 'gainst us; we
Must fly.   So prepare.   Yes, accompany
Thy husband   'Tis a mark of fortitude
Which maketh thee beloved; and 'twill tone and
Vivify the drear thou pictur'st.   Virtue
Shall thus be made to animate, and thou'lt
Not stand the full burden of this transit.
Come, friends, make speedy preparations; for
Apprehension were the synonym for
Death !   [*Exeunt all but* DAVIS.

   DAVIS.   Hope, 'tis a squalid mock; its eye is out.
Oh, metamorphosis!   Tears ?   No!   Arid
Grief's barrenness ;—such grief.   Grief lubricate
Rolleth emotions smoothe, bringing quiescence ;
But this grief's rusty.   It grateth on its
Bearings.   Ah, snap, brain; thou hare-brain!   In-
    ward
Whirlwinds disengage thy roofing.   Rafters
And plates are metal; lead, dull, thick!   Sight too
And hearing.   Alive, yet buried !   Ere my
Clay is cold. forgotten.   I'll nestle down
And die.   Ah, devils throng my tomb.   I dare
Not die.   Oh, were 't welcome !   Shake off thy spell,

O incubus ! Thy shadows scatter, ere
Thou pall'st my heart to stillness. I dare not
Die. Contrast? O human genius, thou canst
Not contrast. Crystal—opaque; white—black; or-
 der—
Confusion; Heaven—hell ! Stale antipodes !
Contrast ne'er flourished till it found acme
In my bosom. It had its birth, its growth,
Its hell feast, within this half hour. I must
Let it play ;—its stage, my blasted hopes; Its
Scenery, ambition's pictur'd glory ;
Its anthem, fate's ogling veto ; its
Audience, sneering humanity; its
Subject, the glory—the grave of Davis !
Man clam'ring wild plaudits o'er his debut
Successful, and framing bright stars from his
Catastrophe. O man, I curse thee, since
I cannot rule thee; and I would fain crush
Thee and dance upon the turf that mark'th thy
Burial place !   [*Exit.*

Scene IV. *A swamp in a forest. Twilight.*

Enter Guide. and negro.

GUIDE. Here is a shady tent ground. Clear
 these bones
Away. Beneath the sullen umbrage of
This palmetto they'll burrow for the night.
 [*They work at clearing the ground.*]
'Twas hereabouts, poor Sol was murdered by
His master. 'Tis a sad story, as
Testify these bones; the bleached remains of
Blood-hounds he slew before he fell. They say
His strong arm shattered many a dog. Grasping
The braying brutes with Sampson's strength, he'd
 whale

Them round tree and snag, dashing their brains.
Well I remember the shocking legend.
Sol was a faithful slave, but too noble
To brook that tyrant's lash.   Well, here's his skull.
No wonder folks say the place is haunted!
       [*Howls and shrieks of wild beasts, heard.*
Hark! That's no hoot-owl; it's a panther's scream!
Woo-o-o-hoo! Soldiers! A weather beaten
Huntsman and know these woods; yet I'm skittish
As a fawn. What keeps them so? [*Shouts, nearer.*
    Enter pickets and sharp-shooters.

FIRST PICKET. We got afoul a briar bramble.   I
say, guide, d'ye think we're goin' to anchor h'yer?
What bones is these?

GUIDE.   The bones of wolves and dogs.   I'd not
    fetch them
Here, but for some special reasons.   Night and
Storm both overtake us.   The place is wild
And miry sinks surround on every side.
To press on is unsafe.   Come, hurry, guards,
Be lively and pitch your pilgrim tent.
Make all things ready for their drear advent.
      [*Shouting in the distance.*

OMNES.   [*In answer.*]   Woo-o-o-hoo!
    [*Shouts in return.   Exit a guard, who gives
signals alternately with gradually approaching calls.*

SECOND PICKET. The infarnal tigers won't be apt
to foller us into sich a swamp, I reckon.

SHARP-SHOOTER.   Don't you believe yerself.   It
aint often as tham fellers sneaks out uv a danger
an' they sartain wo'nt, when they've got sich game
as Jeff. Davis in the wind.

GUIDE.   Are you sure they are on our trail?

SHARP-SHOOT.   Nobody's sartain uv that much;
hit does'nt stan' ter reason.

GUIDE.   You've had your eye cocked on squirrels instead of enemies, to-day, my skeptical friend.

PICKET. Hush, here they come, tired and torn.

Enter guard of soldiers, followed by DAVIS
and lady, her mother and the children. Officers
ELSAN, REAGAN, LUBBUCK *and* JOHNSON.

MRS. DAVIS. Why have we no fire?
Ough! This is the gloomiest camping ground since
Our flight. Please, soldiers, will you not make a
Cheering fire?

SERGEANT. Certainly, ma'am; we too, have just
arrived.
We got entangled in a mire-bog and
Bramble-thicket and belated. Men, haste.
Bring fagots.

GUIDE. Nay, kindle no fires to-night.

MRS. DAVIS. What say you, guide, no fire?

GUIDE. No fires to-night, your grace.

MRS. DAVIS. We shall dissolve in dampness!
shrivel with
Chills in this woe-stricken morass. Morning
Can never dawn on us alive. I bid
You give us a blazing fire! Why, darkness?
Horrible! How prepare refreshments? We're
Sinking, now, of hunger and fatigue. Is
Your wish that we may starve and perish? Well,
You'll gain't with speed. Oh, this loathsome, fenny
Wilderness! Faint, hungry, weary unto
Death? We cannot sleep; but if we might so
Far forget our troubles, 'twere only to
Be roused by shapes, real or unreal, of
Slimy reptiles, in festoons hanging round,
And issuing their forked tongues from venom'd
Heads which hedge their coiled lengths in, whilst
hissing
Out the deadly puffs between their fangs. Wolves,
Bears and panthers....

GUIDE.   Madam, your mind paints sights unlike-
      ly; but
There's a picture in my fears forbids the
Gleam of fire.   Aye, a picture whose artist
Is no trump of wild imagination.
   DAVIS.   Knave, what pratest thou?   My under-
      standing
Is confounded at this colloquy.   No
Fire?   The slop which filleth thy cranial
Cavern if brains one should denominate,
'Twould be a slander of the genus man!
Sirrah, a fire! Zounds!   But my flesh creep'th like
A crab.   The thought of roosting on this quag
In darkness!
   GUIDE.   You took me as your guide; and I
      have striv'n
To screen you from these dangers, by deed and
Counsel, as best my judgment could.   This my
Last, was based upon a deep respect for
You; also the hidious tone of these
Doom-warrants that I tore from trees, while
Coyly blazing on the queachy van.
                              [*Throws down the papers.*
Sir, you repudiate my services;
Therefore, I'll begone.   Make on your fire and
Rue the consequence.   You'll have a yankee
Guard to-morrow.   [*Exeunt guide and negro.*
   MRS. DAVIS.   [*Taking up the papers.*]   What is't?
Some printed paper.   It seemeth good to
Once again see civilization's gentle
Hand.   Reward!   What?   Bring a light.   I do not
Make it out.   [*She staggers and swoons.*
         Friends restore her while Sergeant reads.
   SERG.   "Reward!   One hundred thousand dol-
lars will be paid to any person or persons, for the
capture and delivery to the proper authorities, of

the body of Jefferson Davis, dead or alive! An-
drew Johnson, Pres't, U. S. A."

DAVIS.   Hounded, even into this quivering
Morass, by hell-dogs!   Oh, my lov'd lady,
Better I had taken thy advice and on
The scaffold canceled my political
Offenses, than pay them in this swamp.   Weep,
Treasure in reserve!   I would not choke thy tears.
Bak'd as have been their fountains, my tears do
Also flow.   Oh, that the river of our
Eyes might waft us quickly to the ocean!
Oh, that the bigness of our sorrow might
Engender wings, mounting us in the air
And crown our exodus!
[*Family all nestle together presenting an affecting scene.*
   MRS. DAVIS.   Oh, my dear husband, mother,
      children!   Be
There no cordial to balm our sorrows?   Not
E'en a ray of light to gray this murky
Gloom!   Heaven's twinkling orbs, have they re-
      fused their
Mild auxiliaries?   Shimmering Cynthia
Closed her vestibule?   Even the glow-worm
Hides her little taper and fox-fires gleam
No more.   Oh, might some livid phosph'rescence
Vouchsafe to warm us with its chilly flame!
Cold, damp and drear have been the dews that fell
Round all our former camps, yet till we lost
Our wan'd escutcheon's talisman—our hope—
Was then, to now, a walk in bowers
Elysian.   O diadem, rich in gemmy
Joys!   Thou telescope, that peereth through the
Haze of man's adversity bringing love's
Voids to reck'ning; mirroring on speculum
Joy's smiling views.   Hope!   Exhilarating
Dream of comfort; thou, of all passions most

Essential in this our weight of gloom; thou,
Too, forsaking us?

 DAVIS. Hope! 'Tis that traitor has allured us
   here
And leaving us benighted. joins the mad
Foll'wer. He'll do his work, my shaking knees
     [*A musket report heard. All startled.*
Affirm. Ah! They come. Let me escape. I
Fly! Come to your papa, children, and you,
Dearest, embrace me ere I totter forth.
Jove will retrench his knitted fury, his
Vituperating scowls, and calm the storm;
When I, the object of his wrath, am gone.
They're coming. Where's my horse? Quick, quick,
   where did
I leave him? [*Volleys of musketry. *DAVIS *makes
an effort to escape from the tent, but is privented by
    his friends.*]

 MRS. DAVIS. No, don't go; it is too late. I
   hear their
Footsteps. Mercy, mercy! What shall we do?

 DAVIS. I must not be taken; here, let me kill
Myself! [*Aside.*] I cherish life. [*Aloud.*] I'm
   pausing for
Thy sweet counsel. 'Tis a fearful moment!
I have it. I'll don the female attire!
Be a woman. Will they chase a woman?
Capital hit! Aye, give me crinoline.
Quick, quick, be quick! There; how's that? **Do**
   I seem   [*She assists him.*
She enough? Ah, 'tis a most captious point.
Beautiful. Now, where's my bonnet? There, that
Adds femininity; caps the climax.
Women are guardian angels. Now, ladies,
If this deception save me, though among
Men I lose my scepter, among women

I shall reign a king.   Courage! Here come the
Yammering hell-cats!   Heavens! My nature
Quails.   I'm dragged to execution.   Get me
My weapons.   Aye, ye moles!   What, grinning at
My pain? What but my straits provoke those flips
Of blinking and quaquaversal tricks of
Nose and mouth? 'Tis my distress; my garb: my
Attitude!   Toads! Ye toadied in rhaps'dy,
Like gambling flunkies which lose their cast, while
Your suckers could leech the public dugs; and
Croaked your servile wind-bags on my rise and
Glory; now, ye'd tantalize me with your
Driv'ling grins? Ghosts forefend! I'll scrape your
    skulls
With cleavers!

   Serg.   [*Aside.*]   Cleavers!   He's changed his
     sex; and scolds 'bout knives and
Dishes.   Oh, that she'd get us up one good
Square meal before she goes; snake's eggs, or frog
Soup, broil'd lizard, even a ragout of
Rattlesnake, or a fried tarantula—
Anything, rather than my scanty culm.

   Davis.   What grumblest thou? Of snakes? My
     lady, I
Do loathe the plunging into darkness to
Be mured in gulping solitude.   Wild beasts
Have no respect for sexes, have they?

   Serg.   You're out of danger.   They are afraid of
Scarecrows.

   Davis   How's that? Villain, I overhear it; call
Me a scare-crow?   Out!   [*Chasing him out.*
              Upon my word, I
Think I'd make a better kitchen girl, or
Nurse, or milk-maid, or female rag-picker—
Anything, faith, would I perform with more
Alacrity, than a retreat across
This quavering labyrinth of quagmire.

My gown, it tangles with my legs and whips
Like tail of black-snake. Verily, 'twill hang
Me on some thorn, ere wide I wander. Well,
I'd better be impaled by nature's spears
Than man's. O wretched man! Thou fallest in
Thy dying, on thy sword which gasheth less
The body than the soul! I register
A life's synopsis, then make the final
Plunge: A birth amidst the lowly, yet of
Noble stirps. A thorough, but indulged
Education. A flattered and inflam'd
Ambition. A brilliant and fortunate
Career. A Senator, first Consul, King.
Then, on the zenith shone a glory bright,
Whose sheen did dazzle the wondering eyes
Of men. A name that shot its accent o'er
Hill and valley; o'er rill and river, lake
And ocean; familiar on the deep and
In the household. A name that wrought a sense
Of sympathy with friends, terror with its
Foes. There came a cloud; a storm terriffic.
The sand foundation of this greatness broke.
The gilded fabric fell. Fortune dissolved
To be re-crystalized upon the glaive
Of enemies. Flight. The wilderness. The
Fireless tent. Pursuit. Disguise in female
Habit, and retreat. Hunger and vengeance,
Twin ogres of distriumph now glut their
Appetites, and all but mem'ry's gone. Ho,
Hark! They come. Give me you bucket. Gentle
Friends, adieu!

Enter JOE, *with soldiers, who surround the tent.*

[JOE *approaches the man in disguise.*

JOE. Hey, dey, what have we h'yer? I say, ole
woman, wich away?

DAVIS. [*Imitating a woman's voice.*] I'm going

to the spring. Don't stop me; I'm getting supper.

JOE. Say, yeuw, a purty time uv night, fur ter fetch water, aint hit? H'yer....

MRS. DAVIS. You are uncivil, sir. Would you prevent
A poor old woman from getting water
For the evening meal?

DAVIS [*Trying to wriggle by.*] Don't hinder me, good sir; I want to go to the spring.

JOE. I guess I've seed yer afore! [*Lifting the frock with bayonet.*] Boots! boots! [*Seizing him.* Baird on yer chin, ole lady. A purty woman! I thort I know'd yer!

DAVIS. Stand off! Would you insult a woman?

JOE. That ar's the time her woice grated, like, right smart agin' 'er baird. Marm, now jess yeuw drop hit inter yer boots.

DAVIS. [*Natural voice.*] Keep off from me. Never dare lay hands on me; a man like me!

JOE. Hey, thar, yo make a mistake agin; no man likes yo, nur womern nuther, arter this; fur yeu 'm a disgrace ter thar petticoats. A man like yo! A womern, yo means! Haw, haw, haw, haw! All men yeu've disgraced an' brung ter shame an' now yo warnt ter disgrace all wimmern. Haw, haw, ho! They'll spit on yo. I've seed yo afore. Haw, haw. Oh, my sides! How are yeuw, Jeff? Wal, boys, this yer's rich. How are yeuw, Jeff? Don't ric'lect a meetin' uv me right smart, wonst in the ole Libby prison. I reck'n as how yo don't!

DAVIS. I supposed your government too magnanimous to seize upon a defenseless woman, with her children, in their own camp.

MRS. DAVIS. You had better not lay hands upon his excellency; he might hurt somebody.

JOE. Ho, h'yer we've a defenseless womern with

a nine barl'd shootin' iron an' a pair o' breeches an'
boots on.   Whar's yer night-cap, granny?

DAVIS.   Stand off!   Don't put your hand on me.

JOE.   Ye're easy game.   H'yer, feller soldiers,
h'yer's ole king cotton.   Hit takes a king fur te git
'imself in calico.   Times is changin', like; hit takes
a king fur ter make a womern, these days.   Many
is the honester womern than 'im, as kin kerry high
sail without hevin' ter brag of her cotton.   [*Enter*
FLORENCE, *as corporal in the pursuing forces.*]   I
say, sogers, I'm not in need uv any help; but ye
know thar's a right smart o' bounty on that ar pos-
sum an' ye must all pitch in fur ter arn yer shar uv
hit.   Yo see, the scalp uv king cotton, wich is the
scalp uv a female cotton-bale, wich is the king rooster over all these h'yer male an' female runaways, is
quoted on Uncle Sam's bulletin, at a hundred thou-
and uv money; more 'n I'll want ter use in the tail-
ins uv my life.   So, wade in, boys, ivery skin on ye
an' arn yer shars.   [*They bind him.*

DAVIS.   Be off!   I shall protest against this usage.
Let me loose!   I protest against this arrest.   I call
you, my soldiers and friends, to help me!   Help!
Help!   [*Soldiers capture and*
         bind all males of the Confederate party.

JOE.   I 'spose ef I war a mind ter do that much,
an' wanted ter take adwantage uv my power, like
yo did your'n a cudgelin' an' a doggin' me, when I
war in Libby prison, I mought have yo a danglin' te
yen tree in a jerk o' no time.

DAVIS.   I know you, sir.   I expect no mercy.
The only mercy I do crave is, that
My death be gentle.   Do not torture me.
I plead not to be starved or left to dread
Neglect in dungeon.   Give me a mild and
Quiet death, and soon; for my reverses

And great tortures have unstrung me and my
Nature has fallen into a syncope.
I am prepared to die.

JOE. Wal, I've got no notion uv killin' yo; as I
mought; but yer humiliation tetches me an' melts
my ferocity. Besides, ole Abe wuz kind uv magnanimous like, an' tender hearted, He would'nt hurt
a har on yer head; an' him bein'.a friend uv mine, I
reck'n I'll jess chuck yo inter Fortress Monro ontil
this yer squabble for the darkies' liberty's good an'
settled an' then we'll all vote fur te turn yo out ter
grass an' be a good christian by a lesson yo larned.

FLOR. My brother, you know me not, though I
          have
Been your anxious, watching sister, through all
These dark years of war; and worked my way, as
Female nurse attending to the wounded
And the suffering, as bearer of mails
And of dispatches; even have I risked
My tiny life, performing desperate acts
Of cunning, as a spy, that I might meet
And share my pains with you. You represent
The rough and growing life of the domain
Of higher freedom; and I, its captious
Youth. Do you remember me? We're of a
Common parentage, though torn asunder
At my babyhood, by the unkind feuds
Which rested on the partage of the old,
Paternal home, now grown most opulent.
Fate wrested us apart; I, to be dolled
And flounced in finery and sent to school,
You to range the wild wilderness, we knew
Not where. Do you remember Florence, Joe?

JOE. Wal, now, I reckoned there wuz somethin'
a follerin' uv me round what put me in mind o' my
mother. Sis, by the great grizzlies! Give us yer

leetle pat, my own purty sister. Yo've got a heart
in yo wat's too noble fur ter let yo stay thar, on a
nigger plantashin an' see yer own mother's overseer
pound an' drive an' sell honest folks kase they happen ter be poor an' black or brindle. I've fit fur an'
got a right smart uv a cage wich wants nothin' but
a bird; ye're invited fur te go hum with me. I've
chased 'amost ivery sort uv game, I hev, atween
the Virginny coast an' the Rocky mountains; an'
I 'low, I've seed some pesky queezin' tussles, in my
day, an' the last varmint bagged war Jeff. Davis.

FLOR. And that ends this bloody, cruel war. It
has put an end to this slavery we both abhor. Yes,
brother, I will never leave you.

JOE. Good! Come, men, pick up the traps. We
must git out an' sleep in the clearin'. Hit's too pizen h'yer, fur people wearin' wimmern's clothes. I
cal'late fur te take as good keer uv these poor, shiv-
erin' wimmern as wot I'd take uv my own mother.
Now, pet, yo rogue, yo kin git clar uv tham galant-
in' corp'ral's duds an' we'll hum an' be happy. Many a brave one's bit the dust, but our kentry's free.

Exeunt omnes; prisoners marching under guard.

SCENE IV. FORD's *theatre, Washington.*

A troup of actors, performing a comedy.
Enter the LINCOLN *family and friends, between scenes*

FRIEND. It was most properly devised.

LIN. Yes, 'tis a pleasant recreation, which,
I find, untangles many a snarl of
The confusions into which my mind is
Thrown, on questions of the state. Of comic
And farcical performance, I am fond.

[*They advance and take seats in box. Act progressing.*
Enter THUG, *who impudently surveys* LINCOLN, *then*
walks out, muttering to himself:

THUG. [*Aside.*] Ah, here's a chance! My impa-
tience at this
Dally well nigh runs to frenzy. But the
Auspicious hour has come, for tyrants to
Rue the assassin's stroke. Darkly! The steel?
No. Time were engulfed and observation
Challenged, in effort of the draw
And plunge of knife or bludgeon—precludes one
Trick on risk's desperate gambling table,
Chancing to an escape;—might swash my own
Dest'ny over to this hog-eyed rabble
Who should turn the ordeal booked in fate's
Gamut, against a sweet exit. No, no!
This plot's too deep. Ah, the tug of this blood
Letting bears a tension on the strings of
Courage! Puts brain and brawn awhizz, cyclone
Like! But there's comfort; for the after fawns
The more god-like in honor and reward.
No. 'Tis the dispatch of judgment, to risk
The barking fire-arm's detonating shock,
Which paralyzes thought; then force escape,
Amid the lull of terror. [*Returns and fires.* LIN-
COLN *sinks and is caught up by friends, whilst as-*
assassin escapes, shouting "sic semper, tyrannis."

At same moment, on another part of the stage,
there is portrayed, in tablaux, a scene of the Secreta-
ries' attempted assassination by a band of murderers.

MARY. What has yonder fugitive shadow of
Erebus committed?
OMNES. Assassin! Assassin! A murderer
Has shot the president!
MARY. Oh, cruel, cruel! What has the creature
Done? Killed my best friend? Oh, he is gone and

I'm bereft of all was lovely.　Yet I
Cannot have it.　Impossible!　But now,
He was alive, glowing with animate
Strength.　I do not credit this broad breach that
Yawns 'twixt now and now,　It mocks, it trifles
With, it blasphemes, eternity!　Wake!　Hush!
My answer is my echo.　Hateful fate,
Why was't I too, were not a target to
Th' assassin's eye?　Oh, the green iniquity
Of partial villains!　Return, O awkward
Haggler and re-hash thy crime!

    FRIEND.　Dear lady, do not weep.　The tiger shall
Be caught; for on the vortex of his rôle,
A half the world's agog and the histrion
Shall rehearse it to his cursing minions,
In holes of the infernal, as the king
Of demons!

    MARY.　Oh, bitter, bitter cup!　My life is nipped
Of all the joys which Heav'n had promised.
Long had we buffeted the havoc of
Adversity and tossed 'midst breakers, on
Its madcap foam, together.　Yet spite the
Waves of passion, together we outrode
The awful jar;—calmed its roar to silence.
Even had we begun to talk of sweet
Repose, beyond the glare of public eye
Back in the humble home-dell of our youth.
Repose, next to his Country and his God
Was the ideal of his meditations.
He longingly did prospect on its joys
In life's decline, at home, amidst our lov'd
Ones.　Blessed thought!　Alas!　I trifle with
Realities.　[*Lights slowly fade out.*]　Oh, the dread
        anguish of
My blighted heart!　All nature darkens.　I
Must go with him.　Mate, art not thou trifling

With reality? Awake! 'Tis I. · Wilt
Never listen more? [*She embraces him, weeping.*
 FRIEND. Lady, thy grief's unmeasured; and
  thy tears
Do scald, which course profusely the channels
Of thy years. The blow that smote him, lady,
Is the blow the dying monster slav'ry,
That perished at his hand, raised and darted
With a spasm, at his conqueror. Frothing,
Maddened, convulsed, he rallying, sprang, as
Start'th a wounded lion in his last, mad
Paroxysm, when flesh and spirit sever.
It shocketh, that good and bad should perish
At a breath and with thee, all the world shall
Mourn. But he hath left a name, which, since the
Molten elements from confusion wove
Distinguishable forms; since man, in
Triumph hath swayed distorted chaos; since
Nations rose and fell and giant mind framed
Governments to check ungovern'd passions;
Since language hath lisped tradition or with
Pen made periods historic, hath no
Name out-gloried—a name which hath out-marched
Humanity; fathered new conceptions
Of the possible; brandished the damask
Sword of loyalty to thought, liberty,
Progress; and clove the iniquity of
Property in man which bellowing strove
To smite all justice dead. A name that hath
Set freedom free and rolled off its hugest
Obstacle forever. A name which, though
Its clay embodiment hath fall'n, shall blur
The diamond's glitter; nor tarnish till in
Heav'n all goodness blendeth. See, now! Behold!
The beams of his irradiate name! As
'Twere in yonder apotheosis portrayed—

The rainbow twining round the sun in an
Embrace of raptures!

*Play closes, with a transfiguration scene, embracing
tableaux; also a magnificent stereopticon view of
a panoramic ascension or apotheosis, representing
Lincoln in the arms of Washington.*

Finis.